PRAISE FOR GARRETT LEIGH

"Emotional and brilliant..."

— ALL ABOUT ROMANCE

"Tastefully erotic ... more smart than smutty..."

— PUBLISHERS WEEKLY

"Powerful and compelling..."

— FOREWORD REVIEWS

CHRISTMAS MOUNTAIN

GARRETT LEIGH

PLAYLIST

Last Christmas - Wham!
Woodstock - Joni Mitchell
Sleigh Ride - Ella Fitzgerald
Blue Christmas - Elvis Presley
White Christmas - Bing Crosby
Merry Christmas Darling - Carpenters
Hushabye Mountain - Tony Bennett
Do They Know It's Christmas - Band Aid
Winter Wonderland - Bing Crosby

Listen on SPOTIFY
Link: shorturl.at/ajzMV

1

Rami

Then

I preferred the old name for HMP Manchester. Most days it suited my mood.

But today was different. Life as a probation officer was a thankless one, but sometimes it panned out.

A healthy dose of spring sunshine made the scene playing out before me all the sweeter. Golden rays streamed through the tiny window I found myself glued to as I watched one of my favourite offenders leave the prison, a half empty duffle bag on his back and forty-six pounds stuffed in his pocket. His head was down, shoulders slumped, and I didn't have to see his face to picture the bewilderment in his gaze as he tasted freedom for the first time in years, but I had faith that it wouldn't be too long before he found his place in the world.

A large hand clapped my shoulder. I turned in time to see

the hulking frame of Fen Hawthorne crowding into my quiet corner, a grin stretching his full lips. "Feels good, eh?"

I nodded with a smile that was a fraction of the one splitting his handsome face in half. "This is just the start, though. He has a long way to go."

Fen grunted his agreement, and he may have said more words, but despite my dedication to my job and the offender crossing the street to freedom before my grateful and relieved eyes, Fen's close proximity made me feel some type of way. Warm. Overheated, if I was being honest. And giddy, as if my thrumming pulse belonged to him and him alone. *Strange*ways, you see—the old name for the prison—because given that the only interactions we'd ever shared had been within Her Majesty's walls, Fen Hawthorne did strange things to *me*.

God, he's gorgeous.

And he knew it too. Or perhaps he was psychic and sensed the dizzy turmoil inside me every time we saw each other. Fuck, I didn't even know if he swung in my direction, let alone had any kind of attraction to me. All I knew for certain was that each time I saw him I drove home with a boner I couldn't shift until I'd rubbed one out imagining what lay beneath his uniform.

Charming.

Hey, I'd never claimed to be.

The offender I was tracking disappeared from view. A breath escaped me in a weary sigh. It was early in the day, but this release had been a long time coming. I'd fought for it, tooth and nail, and so had Fen.

He sighed too and turned to me with an expression that matched the cautious and yet apprehensive hope in my heart. "I want him to be okay," he said.

"So do I, but we can't do this for him. All we can do is give him the support system to fall back on if he needs it."

"*You* can," Fen corrected. "With any luck, I'll never see him again."

I felt bad for him then. The offender in question, though quiet, was a character, and I'd hopefully have the privilege of witnessing him come full circle. Fen didn't get that. All he got was an endless goodbye. "I'll keep you updated. I'm seeing him in a couple of days."

Fen nodded. "I'd like that. What are your plans for today?"

"Paperwork, paperwork, and more paperwork."

"Busy day, then?"

"Busy morning. I have to be somewhere else by one."

"Wow. And I thought my job sucked donkey balls."

I laughed, swallowing down a sucking innuendo at the last moment. Conversations with Fen were like that. He seemed to tap into a part of me no one else did and awaken the teenage boy I hadn't been for well over a decade. "I could do without the drive. My car is a piece of shit."

"Get a new one then."

I shrugged. "I don't care enough to spend the money."

"You'll regret that when it breaks down when you need it most."

"Not if the RAC tows me all the way home and I get a day on the couch."

"You'd get the bus." Fen's cobalt gaze drilled into me. "You're way too committed to this gig to bunk off."

I sighed, because it was true. It had to be for the crappy salary I was banking at the end of each month. *It's not the salary that's the problem, it's the child support you're paying for someone else's mistake.* But...no. I wasn't going to think about that right now. I couldn't while Fen was a heartbeat away from invading my personal space. Christ, I could *smell* him. Sandalwood. Trees. Man. It was intoxicating and I wanted to rub my face in it—*on him*—like a wild animal scenting its mate.

Damn, what's wrong with you?

There were too many answers to that question, most of which began and ended with my reprobate brother, but it was a stretch to blame Damon for my overactive imagination. No, that was all me. "You're right," I admitted. "I'd find some way to be here."

Fen grinned again, but it was softer this time and did nothing to tame the lick of arousal warming my blood. "See? Committed."

"And you're not? Pretty sure you've been here all night and your shift ended two hours ago."

"Keeping tabs on me, Stone?"

Yes. "No. Just hard to miss the fact that you haven't slept any time in recent memory." Of course it was hard to miss when a person was as transfixed by Fen's face as I was. The shadows beneath his eyes seemed to jump out at me, and I found myself wanting to smooth them away with the pad of my thumb.

Among other things. Lord, I was on fire today. A wild blaze I didn't have time for, if I was going to leave the prison on time. With immeasurable reluctance, I stepped back from the cage Fen had somehow made around me. "Anyway, I need to get grinding. Enjoy your day, Hawthorne. Get some sleep, yeah?"

I began to move away, expecting to face Fen's blinding grin one more time and spend the rest of the day dreaming of it.

His hand on my arm caught me off guard. His *strong* hand, clamped like a vice around my wrist. "Listen—"

Noise from the nearest wing cut him off. *Loud* noise, shouting, hollering, crashing, and the radio attached to his belt crackled to life, calls for assistance piercing the air as the alarms in the prison began to ring out.

"Damn it," Fen cursed, still holding my wrist. "Can't a dude ask a dude out without getting interrupted by a riot?"

I blinked, half hypnotised by the sensation of him touching me, half blindsided by his sudden contribution to the wicked fantasies I'd incubated since we'd met in this utilitarian hell hole last year. "What?"

"You heard me." Fen tipped me a wink, then turned his attention to whatever was going on somewhere behind him. He released my arm and walked backwards, talking into his radio, before he found my gaze again. "Hold that thought?"

"For how long?"

"All day by the sounds of the ruckus back there. If I don't catch you later, when are you back here again?"

"Wednesday. Pope was my last release, so I'll be picking up some new cases."

"They're lucky to have you." Fen winked again. "Like me, maybe...find me on Wednesday? Unless you don't want to go out with me, in which case I'll accept a flustered middle finger right now."

Flustered didn't even come close, and I only had a split second to react, but there was no way in hell I was ever hitting the reject button for Fen Hawthorne. "I'll find you."

"Wednesday?"

"Wednesday."

Then he was gone, leaving me alone with the abrupt and welcome turn our encounter had taken. For a moment, I stared at the locked gate he'd disappeared through, heart thudding like an overexcited metronome. Then an appointment on my iPad dinged and real life called me home.

Wednesday. It was five days away, and it couldn't come soon enough.

I held onto that thought as the rest of my day played out, and all weekend long, but by the time Monday morning rolled around I knew I wasn't going to make it back to HMP Manchester on Wednesday.

In fact, it was six hellish months before I made it back, and by then everything had changed. My brother was dead and I had part-time custody of his baby son. And Fen?

He was long gone too.

2

Rami

Now

I was an educated professional. I had a first-class degree in criminology and a goddamn-fucking masters on top of the diploma I'd earned while working in the probation service. And yet here I was, scraping jam off my kitchen floor while my nephew screamed blue murder because he was as fed up with me as I was with him.

"I know, mate. I know." I swiped at the sticky mess with a wad of kitchen paper, then decided I didn't care enough to carry on and left it to fester. "Your mum will be here soon. She'll make it all better."

If toddlers could channel cynicism, it was burning strong in the coal-dark gaze of Charlie Stone. He sent a blistering scowl my way and kept crying, and I didn't blame him. I'd been promising his mum was on her way since last night and she still hadn't shown up.

It was slowly dawning on me that she wasn't coming back. That every threat she'd made to me in the last few months was now my reality.

"Having Charlie was Damon's idea. What am I supposed to do now he's gone?"

"Raise him. He's your son."

Leanne shook her head. "He's your brother's son. And he ditched me."

"Damon didn't ditch you. He left, after he caught you having sex with his best friend and you made it impossible for him to stick around without getting killed."

For fuck's sake. How many times did I have to endure this argument?

Too many. And the irony that Damon had died anyway didn't hurt any less than it had eighteen months ago when he'd relapsed and OD'd on a park bench.

Since then, I'd had Charlie part-time while I'd continued to work, but I'd known this day was coming since Leanne had looked me in the eye and flat out told me she didn't give a flying fuck about her son.

Didn't stop me packing Charlie into the car and driving out to search for her, though, and wasn't that two hours of my life I'd never get back? Especially considering I had zero intention of handing Charlie over, regardless of whether she wanted him or not.

You literally just want to call her a cunt.

Facts. And here was another one: I was ill-equipped to be a full-time parent. A few nights a week, I was handling it, but the truth was I was a hot mess trying to keep up with my job and the hundred-and-one other things parenting a toddler came with, even on a part-time basis.

It was 9 p.m. when the cold, hard truth coalesced in my frazzled brain, and I was still driving around Manchester searching for Leanne. Anger deflating, I eased my ancient car to a stop. Charlie had long ago fallen asleep, and I gazed at him in the rear view mirror, my heart pounding as I imagined the next sixteen years with his life in my hands—hands that were currently white-knuckling the steering wheel so hard my coat sleeves had ridden up, revealing the faint scars on my arms from a time where I hadn't managed my own life particularly well. *That was a long time ago.* But it didn't seem to matter how far I'd come since then, as I sat alone in my shit car with my brother's kid snoring in the back, somehow I felt like the same troubled teenager I'd been back then.

I can't do this.

In a daze, I started the car again and drove out of the city, heading north, to the top of the world and the one place I knew I could take Charlie and he'd be safe and loved with family stronger than I would ever be. My sister lived on a goddamn mountain, off-grid and eco-friendly with her husband and three kids. They raised sheep and goats and made fucking cheese in a shed that overlooked a wild and desolate land. Paradise, when the weather was right. A natural prison when it wasn't, but I was familiar with prisons, literal and otherwise.

The tangible interpretation made me think of Fen Hawthorne. Of his ash-brown hair and petrol-blue eyes, always sparkling with humour and mischief. With heat. Or maybe I'd imagined that. It had been so long since I'd seen him it was hard to believe he'd existed, let alone that my god-like memories of him were real.

A flash of pain lanced my chest. I pushed it away, along

with every image of Fen as they tried to bombard my thoughts. Thinking about him hurt more than I could explain, and I had enough pain in my heart to last me a lifetime, or at least the fucking ice age it was going to take me to reach Safia's place in rural peaks of the Cumbrian Lake District.

Because of course it had started to snow.

I whacked my fog lights on and pushed north until the M61 became the M6. In the back, Charlie slept on, leaving me the increasingly loud rattle coming from the car engine for company. Road signs I recognised began to appear, daring me to ignore it and push on. *Don't be stupid. You think the RAC are going to come and rescue you from Durdle Fell?*

The conversation with my more sensible subconscious took me back to Fen Hawthorne again, and this time I lacked the inclination to push him away.

"...my car is a piece of shit."

"Get a new one then."

I shrugged. "I don't care enough to spend the money."

"You'll regret that when it breaks down when you need it most."

"Not if the RAC tows me all the way home and I get a day on the couch."

"You'd get the bus." Fen's gaze drilled into me. "You're way too committed to this gig to bunk off."

Untrue, evidently, as I was due in the office at 7 a.m. for a leadership meeting and there was zero chance of me making it. My saving grace was I had no open cases.

I drove farther north, leaving civilisation behind. The weather worsened, snow pelting down in thick waves of white—well, grey, as it happened, as it was pitch dark on the deserted roads that led to Durdle Fell.

Visibility dwindled to nothing. I slowed to a crawl, leaning forward, and tracked the road as it brought me to the foot of the steep fell, situated in the highest land before England became Scotland, and colloquially known as Christmas Mountain—fitting, given it was the end of November, but light years away from my mood.

I nursed my car along as the grand peak rose out of the vast, uninhabited valley. Save Charlie snoring in the back, I was alone in the dark, a circumstance that had never bothered me before, but with the weight of the starless sky hanging over me, isolation smothered my soul. Could I do this? Dump Charlie on my sister and return to my old life as if it was any better than what Leanne had done to me?

To Charlie, you mean. I corrected the dilemma waging a war in my brain as I eased around a tight bend, the car shuddering over the uneven ground. My heart told me that Safia wouldn't mind one extra tiny mouth to feed, but the closer I got to her homestead at the peak of Christmas Mountain, the more my chest *hurt*, and I couldn't begin to make sense of it. I loved that little boy, but I didn't want to be a parent. I *couldn't* be a parent—not permanently, stuck in Manchester on my own with no days off.

Then you're as selfish as Damon was when he loaded that hit.

As if my car agreed with me, the ominous clanging grew louder, rattling in time with my painful heart, its discontent shuddering like an awakening beast. Outside, the sky seemed to darken, and my tyres slid on the icy road. Dread filled me, and in a last-ditch effort to distract myself from certain doom I sent my racing thoughts in a complete one-eighty and let Fen infiltrate my brain again. He'd always been good at that. Was good at it still, even eighteen months after I'd last seen him, and *a year* since I'd heard on the offender grapevine that in my absence from the prison he'd been stabbed on the lifer's wing.

Jesus. Just thinking about it made me nauseous, a fact I knew without question, because every moment I hadn't had Charlie on my mind, I'd thought about it. About *him*, and the reality that the vague horror story I'd heard in the smoking yard of HMP Manchester was all I knew of his fate, save the fact that he'd been hurt gravely enough to quit his damn job. A job he *loved*. Not that he'd ever told me that, but I knew. I could tell. I'd worked with dozens of prison officers, and they didn't come more compassionate and kind than Fen.

Doesn't mean you knew him, though. I mean, sure, we'd worked on the Pope case together, and our gut feelings on it had aligned, but what else was there? A couple of flirtations over locked gates and bad coffee? *Dream on, Stone.*

I wish. The trouble with dreams was that they didn't take long to descend into nightmares. The images of Fen's smiling face morphed into one of him bleeding out on the grimy floor of a prison cell. I flinched, and my wanker of a car chose that moment to give up entirely.

The engine sputtered and it juddered to a stop.

"Fuck!" I slammed my hands on the steering wheel, waking Charlie.

His startled wail pierced the air.

Cringing, I reached back to comfort him with one hand and rummaged for my phone with the other. I hadn't told Safia I was coming, and she was going to be just *delighted* with me for dragging her husband down the mountain to rescue me in his pick-up truck.

Not.

I found my phone. Swiped at the screen with my thumb.

Nothing happened.

Literally nothing. It was dead, and in my panicked haste to leave Manchester behind, I'd neglected to pack a charger, or, indeed, anything that wasn't in the overstocked bag Charlie took back and forth between my house and the city centre doss house Leanne called home.

Fuck. Actual panic began to replace the irritation singeing my nerves. I gave Charlie a carton of juice and got out of the car. My vintage Adidas crunched on snow and ice as though I was in fucking Greenland not rural England, and my heart surged higher in my throat. Jesus. It was a goddamn white-out. How had I not noticed while I'd been picking my way up the peak?

The answer to that was simple: I'd been too busy drowning in self-pity and thinking about Fen Hawthorne's killer shoulders, and now I was stranded on a deserted, snow-slick mountain road with a toddler and a dead phone.

So do something about it. In my head, I reinvented myself as the kind of dude who carried tools in the boot of my car and popped the bonnet to look at the engine. It whistled in greeting, expelling a gust of steam from the burst radiator hose. I was no mechanic, but I knew enough about car engines to judge that without tools or at least a roll of gaffer tape, it was fucked until I could get it into my brother-in-law's capable hands.

Which wouldn't be any time soon, given that he had no idea I was floundering halfway up the bastardy mutant hill he called home.

The mountain heard me take its name in vain. Icy wind whistled past my ears and it dawned on me with a kick to my already thundering pulse that a broken-down car was the least of my worries. It was *freezing,* and I was stuck in the middle of nowhere with a toddler to keep safe, no passable route up or down the fell, *and* no source of heat to keep him warm until someone—anyone—came upon us. *That could be days. Safia and Paddy won't come down in this and who the hell would be stupid enough to drive on this road in a snowstorm?*

Me, apparently. The same arsehole who'd declared himself a better parent than the flaky piece of shit Charlie had for a mother. *Don't call her that. How many offenders have you seen turn their lives around?*

Lots. But I'd met plenty who hadn't too. Some people were bad to the bone, and I'd been around long enough to know the difference.

Not that any of that mattered right now.

Another gust of wind seared the exposed skin on my face. I shivered and wrapped my coat tighter around me as I considered my options.

After a moment's deliberation, they came to a sum total of one: sit in the car and pray for a miracle. If I'd been alone, I might've chanced trudging up the road in the hope of making it to my sister's place before I was up to my knees in snow, but there was no way I was taking Charlie out of the car until I had a warm place for him to land.

Optimism at its finest, but I had nothing else. I shut the car bonnet and rounded the car to crawl into the back, leaning forward to flick the hazard lights on for as long as the battery lasted. Charlie had cried himself back to sleep. I tucked him up in the spare blanket I kept in his bag and rescued his juice carton, glad the tiny fraction of me that was a sensible human being had packed a few extras, some water, and some snacks. Could a child survive the end of the world on raisins and Ribena? I guess I was about to find out.

I couldn't contemplate a reality where I would fall asleep

with a snowy apocalypse bearing down on me and my two-year old nephew, but somehow I did.

A knock on the window roused me sometime later. Bleary-eyed and disoriented, I raised my head, half convinced I'd imagined it. Then the knocking came again, accompanied by a gruff voice with the kind of timbre that in any other circumstances would've warmed my chilled blood.

I rubbed my face and sat up, peering through the misty glass at the hulking shape outside. My city boy senses told me to open the window and see who the hell it was before setting foot outside of the car. But logic argued that the chances of an axe murderer climbing a mountain just to slaughter us were pretty fucking slim. It was a lot of effort for a tiny blood bath. It was Paddy. It had to be.

Fuck it. I opened the door and stood my wrecked trainers into the snow, sinking up to my calf.

Cursing out loud this time, I came upright, focussing on the tall, broad-shouldered angel who was looming over me, his piercing gaze tight with worry. His piercing *cobalt-blue* gaze that was nothing like the emerald-green that belonged to my brother-in-law.

Damn. How long had we been here? I shook my head to clear it, but all that brought me was the coalescing of the handsome features I'd dreamed about all the way here. High cheekbones, thick brows, and full lips that would've been amazing wrapped around my—

A large hand clamped around my wrist. A *strong* hand, with a vice-like grip that sent my pulse rocketing into my ears, slamming it into my eardrums. I darted a rapid gaze between the scalding hand and the chiselled face my every fantasy was made of.

No. It couldn't be.

But it was.

Unless my nap in the snow had sent me delirious, my knight in shining armour was Fen-Fucking-Hawthorne.

▲

Fen

It was the whisky. I'd barely had a nip—my dad would've called it a dram—but there was no other plausible explanation for the sinfully attractive streak of muscle and bone that had climbed out of the steamed-up, snowed-in Ford Fiesta blocking my gate.

Bloody whisky. It had always set me wrong. I'd only drunk it to take the edge off the restlessness the falling snow had let loose in my soul. Heavy snow round these parts meant one thing: *nothing*. As in, my whole life ground to a halt, no ups, downs, or anything in between, and the impassable road the stricken car was stuck on was a case in point.

At least, I thought it was. With my mind awash with chocolatey hair and eyes the colour of sunshine through a glass of dark whisky—ha, irony—I was having trouble pulling a sensible thought together.

I blinked hard, hoping I didn't look like a serial killer, and glad my neck was covered. My body was less imposing than it once had been, but I was still a big bloke looming out of the dark. If I was the one stranded—

"Fucking hell."

The coarse phrasing, wrapped around a soft London accent, cut through my meandering thoughts. I blinked again, shaking my head as if I'd just emerged from a long swim underwater. I knew that voice as much as I knew the face.

No. It can't be. You're seeing things.

Hearing things.

Whatever. But the harder I stared at the doppelgänger of a man I'd come to terms with never seeing again outside of my overactive imagination, the more solidified the apparition in front of me became.

Rami Stone. Literally the man of my dreams, past and present, because *hell* yeah, I still dreamed about him more than a year since I'd last set eyes on him. A year in which a lot had happened to me and him both, if the longer hair and dark stubble covering his masculine jaw were anything to go by.

I opened my mouth as a gust of wind blasted through the dip in the road that had done for Rami's car. Whatever genius response spilled from my mouth was carried away. More snow fell around us, dotting Rami's hair. He had no hat on, and the jacket hugging his lean build stood no chance against the wild weather bearing down on us.

Get a grip. Whoever this is, they need to get out of the snow as much as you do.

I reached for Rami's other arm.

He evaded, shaking his head. "What the hell are you doing here?"

"Me?" The power of speech returned to me before my brain caught up. "Dude, you're blocking my drive. Don't you think I'm the one who gets to ask the questions?"

Rami frowned, deep and disturbed. He gazed beyond me, up the mountain road, and then back the way he must've come. His rosy lips parted, but nothing came out.

Get him inside. The responsible adult in me finally kicked in. I was still gripping Rami's wrist, reeling from the sensation of touching him again after all this time, despite the fact that his flimsy coat stood between me and his bare skin.

I pulled myself together and gave him a light shake. "None of that matters right now. Just come indoors, okay? Get out of this cold."

Underlining my instructions, I tugged him away from the car.

He fought me, digging his trainers into the snow. "Wait. I need to get Charlie."

The first thing that came into my head was that he had a dog on the backseat that was far better behaved than the collie cross I'd lost a month ago, and that I vaguely remembered him mentioning a dog once upon a time. Maybe. Most of our encounters had involved a serious amount of me losing myself to his twinkly eyes and sardonic smirk.

I let him go.

He spun around, ducked into the car, and a minute later stood tall with...a toddler on his hip.

My eyebrows shot up, taking half my face with them. In the dead of night with the yellow light from my torch to guide me, I could see the little boy had dark hair, and dark eyes like Rami's.

Holy...I searched my brain for memories of him mentioning a child, but there were none. Never. I'd had no damn clue.

Stunned into silence, I took hold of his arm again, relieving him of the bag he'd slung over his shoulder, and guided him away from the stricken car. He didn't lock it, and I didn't correct him. It wasn't going anywhere, and neither was he any time soon.

The thought alone was enough to send my head spinning. Whisky haze forgotten, I steered him through the gate his half-buried car was blocking, past the rope swing I'd swung on as a child, and up the narrow driveway that led to my house. It was a short walk, but into the wind. My face was numb by the time we reached my front door, and I knew any questions I had would have to wait while we got the tiny boy safe and warm.

I shut the door behind us and pointed to the living room where the wood stove was lit. "There's a guard if you're worried about him wandering around. Bathroom down the hall if you need it. I'll get the kettle on."

The whisky bottle was on the kitchen counter. I took my coat, boots, and hat off, and considered offering Rami a drink of the hard stuff, then figured he probably had other things on his mind.

I boiled the kettle and made tea, remembering from the few cuppas we'd shared at work that he took his strong and rosy, just a drop of milk. Good man. I was the same, though, thanks to how brutal life on the mountain could sometimes get, I'd regressed to having a couple of sugars since my time at HMP Manchester. Manual work meant I needed the calories. The gym bunny I'd once been shuddered in horror, but I found far more joy in a mug of builder's brew than I had tubs of protein powder, so I didn't much care.

"It really *is* you."

Rami's low voice—*man, that voice*—made me jump. I spun around. He was right behind me with the pyjama-clad toddler in his arms, thumb jammed in his mouth while Rami nuzzled the top of his head with his cheek. It was quite the picture and my heart stirred, warmth and longing flaring, along with the bright lights of the connection we'd once had. "How old is your son?"

"What?" It was his turn to blink in surprise.

"Your son," I said gently. "How old is he?"

Rami held the boy tighter. "He's not my son."

"So what are you doing up here with him in the middle of the night?"

Rami shot me a sharp look. "Worried I stole him?"

A short laugh escaped me. "Should I be?"

"What do you think?"

"I think I'm hallucinating because you being in my kitchen makes no sense."

"Can't argue with that." Rami drifted forward and peered at the tea I'd made, selecting the one without the sugar as if we encountered each other like this every day.

He backed up. My heart somehow followed him, but I made myself stay put. "Tell me what's happened," I tried again. "Make it make sense."

Rami set his tea back on the table and tightened his arms around the sleeping boy. "This is Charlie. My nephew. I'm taking him up to my sister's place."

"Up?" I computed the simple words and matched them to the only woman I knew who lived anywhere remotely *"up"* from our current location. "You mean Safia McCade?"

"She was Safia Stone once upon a time, but yeah, that's her."

If I'd thought my world had turned upside down ten seconds ago, *man*, it had nothing on the chaos going on right now. I eyed the child again and shook my head. "He isn't Safia's son—oh. He's Damon's, isn't he? She told me about him."

Rami flinched. "You know my family?"

"Of course I do. They're my only neighbours."

Disbelief crossed Rami's face, and I knew the feeling. The plot was thickening by the second and I suddenly longed for the whisky bottle again.

Rami shifted Charlie to his other shoulder. I studied their shared dark features and sadness washed over me. If I'd matched the right information together, then the little guy's father—Rami's brother—was dead.

"I'm sorry, dude," I said quietly.

Rami shrugged. "It was a long time coming."

"How so?"

"Lots of reasons. Drugs. Gang stuff. Everything you, uh, used to see on a daily basis."

I caught his slip, and it was my turn to flinch, but I didn't want to get into all that now. Or ever, actually. Despite everything I knew about recovery and rehabilitation, I'd learned the hard way that talking about the same old stuff over and over and over just made it worse. Things happened and life moved on. Or you died, like Rami's brother. "I'm sorry it affected your family so badly. Safia never told me the details."

"OD," Rami said absently. "Like I said, it wasn't unexpected, just..."

"Awful?"

"Yeah. What about you?"

"What about me?"

Rami eyed me over the top of Charlie's head. "I've told you how I came to be here. You want to return the favour?"

"I live here."

"How? Why? The last *I* knew, you lived in the new-build flats behind the retail park."

"Never said it was home, though, did I?"

"So what was it?"

"My life back then. This is my life now."

"Vague."

"Didn't know you were so interested."

A faint smile warmed Rami's tired face. He averted his gaze, spotting the armchair in the corner of the kitchen by the bookshelf.

He crossed the room and gently deposited Charlie. I followed and pulled a blanket from the basket. It was thick wool and somehow smelled of my long dead grandpa's Christmas cinder toffee. I smelled cinnamon too, but I knew that was all Rami Stone. Cinnamon and mystery, that was him.

Rami straightened, starting when he found me behind him. "I forgot how light on your feet you are for a fucking giant."

"I'm, like, two inches taller than you."

"And a foot wider."

"Not anymore."

Rami's hot gaze spread through me like wildfire. "No, I guess you're not. I didn't notice before."

I nodded and handed him the blanket, then backed up to give him room to tuck Charlie in. I missed his scent, though. There was something so comforting about it, and yet so thrilling it scared me.

Rami left Charlie to sleep and came back to the kitchen counter.

I pulled a stool out for him. "You hungry?"

"Nah."

"Sure about that? You don't look like you had time to eat dinner."

"How can you tell?"

"Instinct."

"Fail-safe, are they? Your instincts, I mean?"

Not even close. But Rami *was* close, and somehow that made the flash of disquiet in my gut, the ripple of fear, easier to ignore. "Look, all I'm saying is that I didn't have my second dinner yet, so if you want to join me there's plenty."

Rami's weary smile returned, lighting up the world like the twinkling young Christmas tree his sister's kids—*wow, that's insane*—had helped me decorate. "'Second dinner'?"

I smacked my stomach. "I'm a growing boy."

"Thought you'd shrunk?"

"Exactly. Need to work harder, don't I?" I didn't wait for an answer. I moved to the fridge and inspected the contents. Given that our geographical location was a hot spot for disruptive weather, I had a loaded freezer that could sustain a small army, but the snowstorm raging outside had caught me off guard as much as it had Rami. It was as random and unpredicted as he was, and my fridge shelves showed it.

I rummaged up ham, festive chutney from the village, and a lump of the cheese his sweetheart of a sister bestowed on me every time she came down the mountain. My prized possession was the sandwich press I'd brought home with me from Manchester. It was a lazy bloke's dream, and when it came to catering I had a gold star certificate in the lazy stakes. I mean, I liked to eat, but I didn't appreciate doing much to make it happen.

The cast iron press heated up while I threw a couple of sandwiches together.

Rami drank his tea and watched, his smile growing a touch, making his dark eyes seem liquid and endless.

"What about the bairn?" I pointed at Charlie. "Is he going to need a snack?"

Rami shook his head. "He'll sleep until I try and put him back in the car."

"That's not happening any time soon."

"Gonna hold me hostage over a sandwich?"

"Not me. The weather. Even if your engine wasn't screwed from a busted radiator hose, that road is blocked in both directions. No soul is getting up or down until the sun comes out to play and trust me, that could take *days*."

Rami blinked, digesting everything I'd just chucked his way. "How do you know about the radiator hose?"

"I forced the catch on the bonnet before I realised you were still inside the car. Figured I'd hot wire it and move it somewhere safer, *and* get it away from my gate."

"Your gate?" Rami seemed mystified, then a light bulb seemed to come on in his head. "Fuck, of course. Hawthorne Farm. How did I forget it was here?"

"Probably because you couldn't see your hand in front of your face in that blizzard out there."

"I still wouldn't have made the connection between this place and you, though. I always took you for a gym rat, not a lumberjack."

"And now?"

"The beard is helping to sway me. It looks good on you."

My hand drifted to my face to stroke the light brown scruff covering my jaw. It wasn't as neat as the dark stubble on Rami's, but I liked it. And I was lazy, remember? Not shaving was awesome.

The sandwich press beeped. I opened it, lifted two golden-brown toasties onto plates, and pushed one Rami's way.

He picked it up, then put it down again. "This is weird as hell."

"The sandwich?"

"The fact that *you* made it. Here, of all places."

A fog between us seemed to shift. I stared at him as if seeing him *right now* for the first time. God, he was right. And it wasn't just weird, it was like somewhere between my front door and his broken car I'd been dropped onto another planet. Or maybe the moon. The silver light filtering through my kitchen window looked good reflected in his molten gaze.

Too good to be true.

Hmm. Maybe it was the whisky after all.

"Fen?"

I blinked. Rami was closer than he'd been before, on the other side of the counter and standing beside me. "What?"

"What do you think?" Rami gestured around them. "Last I heard, this place was run by a dude forty years older than you, though admittedly that was a while ago."

"You don't get up here much?"

He shot me a guilty wince. "I haven't even met my sister's youngest kid."

"Lalla's a sweetheart. Blonde hair like her dad and big brown eyes like yours."

"We get them from my mum."

"I know. Safia told me."

"She's never mentioned you."

"Why would she? I'm guessing you didn't have much call for Christmas trees and firewood in Manchester."

"No, but she knew I spent time at HMP Manchester. If she knew you worked there, she'd have asked us about each other."

Rami's dark gaze bored into me, and I wondered how much he knew. If he was testing me. Or if he was just understandably curious about the macabre event that had brought me back to my family home.

"She never asked me where I was before, and I never told her." I reached for my sandwich and ate half of it in two bites, holding Rami's steady gaze. "I might've done if I'd known she was your sister, though."

"Why?"

I shrugged and ate more food. "Because I missed you."

3

———

Rami

"Because I missed you." Of all the random, head-fucking things that had come my way on this crazy day, why were those four little words the only thing that seemed to make any sense?

Fen hadn't missed me. He *couldn't* have. We hardly knew each other. We'd never exchanged numbers and I hadn't looked him up on social media because no one who worked in the prison system ever had accounts in their real name. We were invisible.

Untraceable.

And somehow we were both here, and...yeah. I'd missed him too.

How? You only saw him, like, twice a month for a snatched few minutes. But it wasn't just him I'd missed. It was the soothing drum beat my pulse became whenever he was close. His warmth. His smile. His playful gaze, even though I was fairly sure he was hiding the fact he didn't want to talk about getting stabbed at work behind his perpetual good humour.

27

Maybe I should've told him that knowing he was alive and well was all I'd ever wanted.

I'd have been a lying fucking liar, though.

I wanted to see him. I wanted to put my hands around his and tell him I gave a fuck.

That I *still* gave a fuck, but my soul was a crowded place right now, and I lacked the spoons to dissect it.

As if he'd heard my heart, Charlie sighed in his sleep. My gaze drifted to him and my mind to the madness that had led him to be curled up on an armchair in *Fen's* kitchen. I wanted to tell Fen I'd missed him. That it was okay if he didn't want to talk about what had happened to him and it always would be, but the words stuck in my throat. Until I got Charlie to the top of Christmas Mountain, he needed my undivided attention.

I put my hand on Fen's strong forearm and squeezed it, revelling in the unyielding flesh that answered me. Then I stepped back and picked up the supper he'd made me. "This looks amazing. Thank you."

Fen nodded and turned away to put his empty plate into the sink. I ate the sandwich in record time and he grinned when he looked back to find it gone. "Knew you were hungry."

"It's that damn fucking cheese. I'd forgotten how much I liked it."

He smiled. "And *I'd* forgotten this about you. Not the cheese, I mean how you speak. Like a sailor in a pub kitchen when you're not being all professional, like."

"'Professional'?" I snorted out a laugh. "I have a meeting in—" I checked my watch—"Four hours and I'm not going to be there. There's nothing professional about me right now."

Fen's grin widened. "You're wrong. I always found it cute

as hell how you'd tear the guv'na apart with big words and mad-long sentences, then call him a twat when his back was turned."

"Maybe I'm just gutless."

Fen glanced at Charlie, then back at me, his eyes darkening like the sweetest storm. "Never."

"That's cute."

"You don't like cute things, Stone?"

I rolled my eyes. "Don't call me that."

"Not denying it then."

His flirtation was as gentle as it had ever been, but in this moment it was somehow lighter, as if he knew in this upside down place we'd found ourselves in, I needed him to be something I recognised.

I played my part. "I never denied it."

His grin morphed into the smirk I'd seen in my dreams more often in recent months than I cared to admit. This was the Fen Hawthorne I remembered—the man with the wicked smile and eyes that seemed to dance no matter the light in the room. Because he *was* the light in the room, especially when his epic gaze snared me like it had right now.

Repressing a shudder, I blew out a breath. We'd come full circle. He was flirting and I was loving it, but the fact remained that we hadn't seen each other in more than a year and here I was, somehow marooned with him in the last place on earth I'd ever have thought to find him. *Life is fucking weird.*

Fen took my plate and dumped it into the sink with his. He seemed to sense I'd run out of brain power and he pointed at the stairs. "There's a spare room up there with a bed big enough for you and Charlie. Why don't you get some sleep?"

It took me a minute to compute that meant going to bed in his house. As if I hadn't quite grasped that it was hell o'clock and my car was fucked, and even if it hadn't been, the relentless snow had probably buried it up to the wheel arches by now. "You're offering me a bed for the night?"

A complex mix of emotions passed over Fen's features, each one too fleeting to catch. "Course I am. And not just because I already know your pretty face. Your sister's been good to me since I came back here. I'd put up any brother of hers."

Not Damon. I didn't say it, though. What was the point? Fen would've given the shirt off his back to a stranger and he didn't deserve my bitter self-pity.

Shit, I didn't either, but bad habits were the hardest to break. "We'll be out of your hair in the morning."

Fen snorted. "Sure you will."

I didn't want to think about what he meant by that. So I didn't. I scooped Charlie from the armchair and tucked him under my chin.

Fen watched me with a soft smile. "I never thought of you as the paternal type, but it makes sense now—all those lags you go above and beyond for."

"You did as much for them as I did. More, most of the time."

A quiet hum was Fen's only answer, and I wanted to go to him, to get up in his face and unpick the complexities clouding his gaze. But with Charlie in my arms I wasn't that man, and the fact that I wanted to kiss him was an extra complication I didn't need either.

I hid my face in Charlie's sweet-scented hair, just for a moment.

When I faced Fen again, his eyes were gentle. Inviting. I

stepped towards him before I caught myself. "Um... goodnight? I guess? Or is it morning?"

"Not quite." Fen stayed where he was and a tense, strange moment passed between us. Then he smiled and the light from the nearby Christmas tree made him look like a bearded, cuddly angel. He closed the distance separating us and cupped my face with his warm hand, his thumb tracing my cheekbone with a gossamer touch.

My heart thudded. I had so many things I wanted to say, but none of them felt right.

I settled for a smile.

Fen smiled back, then let his hand drop as he stepped away. "Goodnight, Rami."

"Goodnight, Fen."

▲

It was the scent that woke me first. Earth and trees. Wood and smoke. Not the diesel and weed that wafted through the vents of my city centre flat.

Then it was the fact that the hot chubby hands I'd fallen asleep with were no longer welded to my face.

Fuck! My eyes shot open, arm flailing out to the last place I remembered Charlie being—fast asleep next to me, snoring like his Uncle Paddy after ten pints.

But Charlie wasn't there. The space beside me was empty and I bolted upright and charged out of the room without giving a single fuck that I was dressed in the jeans I'd passed out in—no socks or shirt.

I flew down the stairs, heart in my mouth, a dozen scenarios playing out in high definition, none of them good.

He's wandered off and fallen down a well.

I forgot him altogether and he's alone in Manchester.

Fen really was a figment of my imagination and the weirdo who lives here has kidnapped my infant nephew.

I reached the kitchen as the last, most ridiculous alternative reality flared in my imagination.

Fen was there, naturally, standing at the kitchen counter, guarding Charlie who sat in front of him eating toast.

Relief swamped me as fast as terror had ten seconds ago. I blew out a breath and leaned hard in the doorway. "I thought he liked square pieces."

At the sound of my voice, Charlie jerked around, dropping the tiny, crustless triangle. "Rama!"

Fen lifted him down from the countertop. Charlie's feet hit the floor and he ran at me like a midget rugby player, tacking my legs with enough force to send me reeling back if I hadn't been smashed in the nuts enough times to be anything other than ready for him.

Laughing, I scooped him up, sensing Fen's gaze all over me as I swung my nephew high, then settled him against my chest. "Where did you go? I thought monsters had eaten you."

Charlie laughed. "Rama!"

"Yeah, yeah." I set him down.

He toddled right back to Fen. "Toast!"

Fen shrugged and hoisted him within reach of his plate. The action seemed easy for him, natural, and with the only light in the room coming from the approaching dawn and his sparkling Christmas tree, he was more beautiful than ever.

"I have bad news for you," he said when my fixation with his soft grin rendered me mute.

"Oh yeah?"

From his resumed post guarding Charlie with his strong

arms, he gave me a steady look. "The snow is set in both ways on that road, up and down, so whatever your plans were, you're stuck with me for a while."

"Stuck with you…" The words left my lips like a prayer. I pursed them shut and drifted to the window, but it was murky enough outside that I couldn't see shit.

"If you want to see for yourself, I put your coat by the back door. Do me a favour, though, and take my boots. Those trainers you rocked up in will give you frostbite."

"Yeah, well I didn't dress for mountaineering, so…"

"Maybe you should've, considering you were driving up, I don't know, a *mountain.*"

Sarcasm usually made me want to throat punch people, but Fen spoke so entirely without malice that it was cute on him. I took his advice about the boots and stamped into the pair nearest the door before I remembered I wore no shirt.

Fen laughed and peeled his thick sweatshirt off his broad, warm body. He held it out. "Don't worry about the boots on the floor. I'd rather a bit of muck on my tiles than drop this bairn."

His Cumbrian accent felt brand new to me, velvet and sweet. It reeled me in. I crossed the kitchen and took the sweatshirt from him, already knowing it would feel amazing against my bare skin.

I wasn't disappointed, but being swamped in his scent left me dizzy.

And perhaps he knew it. He said no more and turned his attention back to Charlie, leaving me to my outdoor recce in peace.

I returned to the back door and put my coat on. It helped with the Fen overload, and I stepped outside with a clear head.

Frigid cold hit me, my borrowed boots crunching on the kind of icy snow I never saw in the city. Pure white and a foot deep, it was almost as pretty as Fen.

I followed his footsteps to the gate he'd led me through in the dead of night, gathering my bearings as my geographical memories came back to me. This magical place was a Christmas tree and timber farm that had been in the same family for generations. Until five years ago, they'd owned all the property on Durdle Fell, then they'd sold the land at the very top to my sister after the death of their patriarch. Fen's father, I presumed, though I wasn't about to ask. On the list of questions I had for him, property dealings between our families were somewhere near the bottom. At the top, was what the *hell* had happened to him to bring him home, but I'd pick my moment for that, and if it never came, that was my problem, not his. I'd die of curiosity before I upset him.

I reached the gate. As promised, the snow was as thick on the road as it was on Fen's property, and my car was still buried and useless. *Fuck that car. Piece of shit.* But even my brother-in-law's truck wasn't making it through the current blizzard, so I was being a little harsh.

Not that I cared. It was a car, not my fucking dog. I trudged all the way to it, swinging my gaze up and down the road as if I could shift an entire weather system with my discontent. Obviously, nothing happened. I didn't even get cold, thanks to Fen's sweatshirt and I walked back to his house warmer than I'd been inside. On the way, I passed a series of gates and paths I now remembered led to the forest, the timber yard, and the big barns. There were snow-topped trees everywhere. A sweeping horizon. Endless skies. It was breathtaking. Beautiful. If I didn't stop to consider that the sparkly aesthetic had taken me hostage it was almost paradise.

Beyond the farm in the distance, lay a bigger house. I wondered who lived there now, or if Fen was an orphan, like me. *Maybe that's why he came back here.* But as logical as that was, I knew there was more to it, and only the fact that my own life had imploded stopped me ruminating my nosiness into a migraine.

I need to call Safia.

I stepped back into Fen's cosy kitchen, and because he was a fucking psychic, he handed me my charged phone.

"You left it on the counter last night. I figured you'd need it this morning."

I grunted my thanks.

Fen laughed. As much as I sensed something different about him, he still did that a lot—laughed with this warm, infectious joy that needled its way into even the moodiest man's personality. I'd seen it in action on the prison wings, the way his presence could make a dangerous landing a safer place just because he smiled like the sun.

I'd missed that. I didn't know much right now, but that I couldn't deny.

"Hey." Fen broke the daze I'd drifted into with a soft elbow to my ribs. "You okay? You never did get around to telling me how you came to be halfway up Christmas Mountain with this little guy."

Charlie was now on the floor, on the rug by the armchair I'd laid him on last night, playing with a felt set I vaguely recognised, which made no fucking sense at all. "Yes, I did."

"Nope. You told me you were headed to Safia's place. Not why you were doing it in the middle of the night with no overnight bag or supplies that weren't for the bairn."

"So, you're a proponent for me *doing it* in the middle of the day?"

A *very* faint flush stained Fen's cheeks, and I smirked. My style of flirting had always been dirtier than his, which was why he'd rarely seen it, as we'd spent the entirety of our friendship at work.

"It wasn't exactly planned," I admitted.

"Sounds like the kind of opening we're gonna need a cuppa for." Fen lit the flame beneath the kettle. "Go on."

I sighed. "You really want to hear my family drama?"

"Course I do. I'm stuck with you for the next twenty-four hours, so you may as well entertain me."

Twenty-four hours. "Dick."

"Ouch. You're a grumpy dude, eh? I always wondered."

"What else did you wonder?"

Fen's smile was...sweet. "Lots of things. Right now, I'm wondering if you slept okay, if you're hungry, and if you want to use the landline to call your sister as the phone signal up here is pants."

"Pants," Charlie echoed.

"It is," Fen agreed. He held my gaze for a moment, then turned to Charlie and wiped his sticky face with a damp cloth. "Do you still want to see the biggest Christmas tree in the world?"

Charlie's eyes grew round. He clapped his hands.

Fen laughed and faced me again. "Is that okay? It's not far from the house and I'll keep him wrapped up in my coat like a newborn."

Every instinct I had told me Charlie was safer with Fen than he was with anyone. More than that, Charlie was *happy* with Fen, after he'd spent the last year screaming every time a stranger had looked his way, a belated realisation that should've occurred to me the moment I'd come downstairs to find them together in the first place. But the fact that I'd spent his entire life trying to keep him safe from other people-induced disasters betrayed me.

I hesitated, and Fen saw it.

With Charlie on his hip, he rounded the counter and came to stand close to me. "Tell you what, why don't you go take a shower and make whatever calls you need from my bedroom. Me and the bairn can watch cartoons until you get back."

His nearness was distracting. I wanted to stroke my fingers through his beard, cup his strong jaw in my hand and—

"Rami."

I blinked. "Hmm?"

Fen's brow furrowed, a tiny frown creasing his forehead. "Is there something else going on?"

"Like what?"

"I don't know, whatever keeps making you zone out like you've banged your head. You're not in trouble, are you? For taking him away from his mum?"

A bitter laugh escaped me before I could stop it. "I didn't take Charlie. She left him with me and didn't come back, like she's been threatening to since he was born."

Fen winced. "Sounds complicated. Drink the tea."

He reached across the counter with his free hand and slid a full mug to me. Somehow, I'd missed the kettle boiling and him brewing up.

"Thanks," I said absently as Charlie put his warm hand to my cheek. It was usually sticky with whatever yuck he'd managed to pick up since the last time I'd mauled him with a baby wipe, but under Fen's care he was clean and dry, and my silent refusal to let them out of the house together seemed even more ridiculous. "It's not that complicated, to be honest. Just fucking shit."

Fen smoothed Charlie's hair. The gesture was affectionate and kind, and for some inexplicable reason made me want to cry when I hadn't shed a fucking tear since I was sixteen years old and my dad died of MND.

I held out my arms. Fen eased Charlie into them and pointed at his living room. "Telly is in there. Don't ask me how to work it, though. Addie has to show me every time he's here."

"Addie?"

"Your other nephew. The DVDs by the wood basket are his."

There was nothing about those words that didn't make my head spin. Fen belonged in the world I'd left behind in Manchester, not holed up in this cosy house with my sister's kids who I barely knew. *How* was this my life right now?

I took Charlie into the living room and tucked him up on Fen's battered leather chesterfield. There were blankets folded on just about every available surface. I snagged one and pretended to steal Charlie's nose from his face.

He scowled. "No."

"No what?"

"No my nose. Is mine."

"It's mine now. I ate it."

"Rama, *noooo!*" Charlie's wail was loud. If I hadn't known him better I'd have thought him upset, but he wasn't. His dark eyes shone with laughter and he beat his tiny fists on my chest. "Nose mine."

I gave it back to him and ruffled his hair, destroying Fen's efforts to tame it. "You want *Octonauts*?"

"Yeah!"

I found Fen's remote and navigated his TV to the CBeebies channel. The theme song for the show that made me want to stick pins in my ears blasted out until I discovered the volume button.

By then, Fen was watching me from the doorway. "And I thought I was a relic when it came to technology."

"Fuck off."

He snorted. "You don't watch your mouth in front of him?"

"Nope. I'm a terrible parent."

"Sounds like he's had worse."

Sighing, I left Charlie on the couch and jerked my head at the kitchen. Fen preceded me back to the counter and opened the fridge, giving me space while I found the optimal position to watch Charlie and ogle Fen's broad back at the same time. "Damon wasn't a bad dad, just messed up. He was getting better in the months before he OD'd."

"Is that why he OD'd? Because he hadn't been using and his tolerance was lower?"

"Maybe. I try not to think about it anymore. Drove me half-crazy at first."

"Man, I'm sorry." Fen threw me a contrite glance. "Tell me to shut up if I dig too hard, okay? I'm too nosy for my own good."

"Is that what this is? You being nosy?" If it was, I wanted a turn.

Fen's only answer was the packet of bacon he slapped on the kitchen counter. "I hope you like sandwiches because I pretty much live on them."

Worked for me. I watched him fry bacon and butter bread while I gave him the short version of how I'd messed up enough to wind up stranded in his house with him for however long it took the road to clear. "It never occurred to me to check the weather. It's been such a chaotic year, I forgot it was even winter."

The lights on Fen's tree changed their pattern, flickering in a rhythm that made my eyes twitch.

Fen chuckled. "You can blame Addie for that too. He couldn't decide which one he liked so we set it to random."

"My nephew decorated your Christmas tree?"

"And your niece. It was payment for the Norway spruce I gave Paddy to haul back up to their place."

"That was nice of you."

"They're nice people."

"I know. That's why I came here."

"To leave Charlie with Safia?"

The bacon was done. Fen fished it from the pan and placed it on the thick bread. He already knew I liked ketchup instead of brown sauce because we'd had that debate on the wing with an anxious inmate, a diversion technique that had worked far better than anything I'd ever learned from a textbook.

He passed me a plate and a bottle of Heinz.

I doctored my butty and pulled a face at the HP sauce he preferred. "That shit tastes like pickled onions."

"And your point?"

"It's disgusting."

"All right, lad. Enjoy your jam on bread."

The familiar exchange almost distracted me from the fact that Fen clearly knew the youngest members of my family better than I did. Then an ornament on the tree caught my eye. It was made of a cardboard tube and had eight faces drawn on it with crayon. Names were scrawled beneath each one: *Mummo, Dadda, Addie, Mae, Uncle Rama, Uncle Damon, baby Charlie, and...Uncle Fen.* He was the last face drawn next to mine, though with the purple beard the artist had given him, I'd never have guessed. Sandwich forgotten, I drifted to the tree and hooked the cardboard tube free from its branch. "How long have you had my portrait hanging in your kitchen?"

Fen frowned. "What?"

I held up the tube, turning so that his face and mine were on full display. "Missed me that much, eh? You could've, like, messaged me for nudes instead."

A beat of silence thudded between us and I wondered if I'd gone too far. For all Fen liked to flirt, he'd never taken it to the gutter. Then he abandoned his own breakfast and crossed the room in two long-legged strides. He took the ornament from me and stared as if he'd never seen it before. "Damn," he whispered. "That's...I don't even know what it is. Addie made this last year—it's why Lalla isn't on it—and I can't imagine how I'd have ever looked at it and thought of you."

"You don't see the likeness?" My tone was dry, because in all honesty, there was none, and ever since Addie had coined me Uncle Rama when he'd been Charlie's age, no other fucker in my family had called me by my actual name.

Fen fell quiet, lost in thought. I moved to take the ornament from him, but as fate was playing hardball today, naturally I missed and grabbed his wrist instead.

My fingers wrapped of their own accord around his strong forearm, but tightening my hold was a conscious choice. It had to be—it felt too good to be an accident. "For what it's worth, I'd have called you if I'd had any clue how to find you."

Fen smiled a soft smile that was as haunted as it was

lovely. "I felt the same once I got back here and put my head back together. The irony that you were etched on that damn trinket all along is killing me."

"Don't die. I need you to make me those banging cups of tea."

"Fair enough." Fen hung the ornament back on the tree. "It must be pretty strange for you to realise I've been around your family this whole time and you had no idea."

"That's one word for it. They've never mentioned you by name, but then, every conversation I've had with Safia in the last...shit, however long this clusterfuck has lasted—has been about Damon and Charlie. It's consumed us."

"I can imagine. I know she was worried about him for a long time. She was worried about you too, I—" Fen shook his head. "Sorry."

"What? What is it?"

"I just wish I'd known it was you. Maybe I could've helped."

"What would you have done? Told my sister I was the bloke you'd been chatting up at work for a year and half and offered to be my live-in manny so I could take Charlie from Leanne before she got a chance to dump him?" It came out in an unpunctuated rush, and louder than I meant it too. "Fuck, *I'm* sorry. None of this is your problem."

"Telling me about it doesn't make it my problem." Fen covered my hand with his and guided me back to the kitchen counter before he detached us. "Eat your breakfast."

I obeyed while he watched me, but it didn't feel as weird as it might've done if I'd had prior warning of this *Twilight Zone* morning. When I was done, he took my plate to the sink in a repeat of our dead-of-night snack. His back called to me again, though I couldn't say why. I liked his face just as much and zeroed in on it the moment he turned around.

"What happens now?" he asked. "With Charlie, I mean. Is Safia going to keep him?"

"That was my plan when I hurled us up here last night, but perspective and a couple of sandwiches apparently do magical things for brain power."

"How so?"

"I have parental responsibility for him—legally, as well as —" I brought my fist to my chest— "you know."

"Safia could get that if it was what you both wanted. He'd have a grand life up here, and she's the best mum."

"I know that."

"So..."

I tipped my cooled tea down my throat. "I don't want to not be his parent, I just—" I closed my eyes, tracking Fen's soft tread as he neared me again.

"It's okay," he whispered. "Whatever you feel isn't wrong and none of this is fair to any of you."

"Don't be so reasonable."

"Don't be so guarded. It's just you and me here. You can say what you need to say."

I opened my eyes. Fen was right beside me, his gaze shimmering with the kind of empathy I'd never seen in anyone else, even the people who loved me most. *He gets me. How I knew after such a short time in his company I had no idea, but it was true. I felt it. Believed it.* "I don't want to do it alone. It fucking scares me."

"Then don't do it alone. Stay up here with Safia and raise him on the mountain."

A half-crazed laugh bubbled out of me. "Yeah, that's not going to work for me."

"Why not?"

"I don't know if you've noticed, but I'm not a man-of-the-mountain kind of bloke."

Fen rubbed my forearm, a fleeting gesture over and done so fast I barely had time to register the wave of warmth left in its wake. "I thought that too, once upon a time, then the world shifted and I found myself back here after fifteen years away. When it hit, it took me a while to reconcile how I felt, but I'm telling you, man, this place is healing. It's magic, and there's no better place to raise a child."

My heart thudded as I sank into his earnest gaze. My lips tingled too, letting me know that if we'd found ourselves thrust together in another context, circumstance, shit, another lifetime, we'd have been kissing the hell out of each other by now. Maybe more.

But I didn't kiss Fen.

And he didn't kiss me. He bumped my shoulder with his big fist, then he left the house and he didn't come back, and for reasons I had no clue how to understand, it felt like losing him all over again.

4

———————

Fen

It took me another twelve hours to figure out that Rami Stone was more emotional than the man I'd had a mad crush on back in the day. By then, it was dark again and I was standing in my kitchen once more trying to figure out how to feed two extra mouths I hadn't in a million years prepared for.

Rami and Charlie were upstairs in the bathroom, where they'd been when I'd come back to the house after a long day on the farm doing the work of ten men with the five who lived onsite and didn't have the excuse of being snowed in elsewhere.

I was *tired*, but kind of buzzing too. Apparently Rami Stone's mere presence was better than coffee.

In an effort to give him and Charlie some space, I'd showered downstairs and dressed in the first clothes I'd found in the utility room, so now here I was, barefoot in my kitchen, staring at a million tins of beans while dressed in old sweatpants and a holey T-shirt with a pink rabbit on it. *Sexy*

45

AF. In another lifetime, if hooking up with Rami had been a genuine possibility, I'd have been worried.

As it was, I wasn't worried. Just hungry and half convinced the last twenty-four hours had been a dream I was about to wake up from. I eyed the whisky bottle on the counter. Maybe if I took a swig the world would go back to how it had been the previous night, when insomnia had driven me to be drinking and staring out of the window in the first place. If I'd been asleep, I wouldn't have noticed Rami's car until morning, and by then, he might've been—

"Fenny!"

Tiny hands pawed at my leg. I bent and swung Charlie from the floor and settled him on my hip, the way I so often did with his cousins. It was autopilot, I didn't give it much thought until I sensed Rami's eyes on me from behind.

I turned to face him. He was in the kitchen doorway, dark hair wet and sticking up as much as Charlie's, wet hand prints on his clothes. "All right?"

He nodded. "Think so. You?"

"Yup."

I went back to staring at the kitchen cupboards while Charlie played with the talisman necklace I wore around my neck.

"Rock," he said.

"It's a rune." I turned it over so he could see the engraving on the other side. "My daddy thought he was a Viking."

Rami laughed. "That makes sense."

"What does?"

"The Viking thing. It suits you."

"I said he thought he was one, not that it was true."

"Okay."

He was laughing at me, I could tell, but I didn't mind.

Rami Stone laughing was a sight to behold, and I abandoned the open cabinet in front of me to lose myself in the way his eyes crinkled at the sides and his rosy pink lips stretched wide. With his head tipped back, his neck had a perfect, elegant arch.

I wanted to bury my face in it, but that craving wasn't new. I'd always found Rami's neck appealing. Below the dark stubble, his skin was creamy and flawless, leading down to shoulders that were sinewy, but corded with muscle. I wondered if the dark hair on his head dusted his chest too, then gave myself a mental kick. *Get a grip. He's not here to be leered at.* Though, I was still having trouble believing he was here at all.

My stomach growled, making Charlie giggle. He poked me. "Monster."

"In my belly?"

He laughed, tipping his head like Rami had, but farther back, trusting me to keep him from hurtling out of my arms and onto the flagstone floor. And he was right to trust me. There was zero chance of me dropping this bairn. As long as he wanted to be in my arms, in my house, in my life, I had him. "Belly monster."

I laughed too, but it cut off when I caught Rami's gaze again. And there it was, the emotion swimming in his dark eyes that made my heart beat too fast. The loneliness, the pain, the distress that had led him to throw this kid into the back of his beat-up car and hurtle up a mountain in a snowstorm.

Charlie wriggled to get down. I let him and he toddled off to the living room as if he'd lived here his whole life. A moment later, the TV blared, and Rami winced. "Sorry. He figured it out on his own."

"I don't mind. It's nice to have some noise around here."

"You don't like the quiet?"

"Sometimes, when I've been with my crew all day, yelling at them over chainsaws and the wind."

"Is that where you've been today? Cutting down trees?"

"We didn't fell any today. Too dangerous with this wind. Spent most of our time hoofing timber around. We have too much since this storm caught us off guard and shut down shipping. Along with the Christmas tree orders, it's going to be crazy round here when we get moving again."

"Busiest time of the year?"

"By far. Coming to a standstill like this feels like a dream."

Understanding flooded Rami's dark gaze. "Know the feeling, mate. Not that my job has ever been seasonal."

"Do you have many cases at the moment?"

Rami cast a glance into the living room, then shook his head. "I went part-time when Damon died. I only take a few at a time now. A couple are in the prison, but most of them are post-release at the moment."

"How's it going?"

"What do you care?"

"Harsh." I folded my arms across my chest. "You think that's a weird thing for me to ask?"

"Unless you're asking about someone specific, then yeah. You know what my job is like. It's not something I want to bring home."

"You're not at home. And I wasn't being specific about an offender, I was asking about *you*."

Rami's face did something complicated. I wanted to decipher it, but he was too quick for me. His expression flattened before I could take a breath, and he offered me a bland smile that killed my appetite. "Fuck, I'm sorry. I'm a moody twat, okay? And there's nothing to tell about work that you don't already know. I do my job and look after Charlie. That's all I am these days."

I didn't believe him. He was built for more than that, and the spiky probation officer I'd known back in Manchester had never treated how he spent his days as just a means to pay the bills. He'd cared, deeply, and he'd sweated blood to make sure the offenders under his wing got a second—or third, or fourth—chance at life. If I'd ever found myself on the wrong side of the barred windows, I'd have wanted him on my side. *That's all I am* didn't apply to Rami Stone.

Still, I changed the subject. "Did you get hold of Safia?"

He nodded. "I did. You were right about the mobile signal, so I used the landline in your bedroom."

Thinking about him in my bedroom was a new kind of wow. I forced my attention back to the cabinet and grabbed two cans of baked beans. "She okay?"

"She is now. Think I blew her mind when I told her that we already knew each other."

I knew that feeling. "She's probably relieved. If she thought I was putting up a stranger on her behalf she'd likely try and give me a whole sheep again."

"A whole sheep?"

"Yeah. Don't worry, it was alive, but my dog chased it back up the mountain before it could get its hooves under the table."

Rami shook his head. "You guys live on another planet up here. I swear down, I couldn't understand most of what she was telling me."

"That's because you're southern and soft."

"So's she. At least, she used to be. Now she's herding goats and breaking rocks with her bare hands. What are you doing in that cupboard? Have you lost something?"

It belatedly occurred to me that I'd been staring into the same cabinet since he'd come downstairs. I shut it with a bang and dropped the bean tins on the counter. "I've got a pie in the outside freezer. Can't say what's in it, but it came from the butcher in the village. That all right for your dinner?"

"You don't have to cook for us, Fen."

He said my name, and his soft tone drew my gaze from the bean tins to his face. My whole body tingled as I fought the urge to inch closer to him. To crowd him against the door where he stood and breathe him in. It was strange as hell to have him here, but ignoring the fact that I wanted him as much as I ever had felt stranger still. "I want to cook for you," I said instead of blurting out the nonsense running through my tired brain. "Makes me feel better about the fact you're stuck here when you need to be with your family."

"I need to be at home, actually. At work, while Charlie's at nursery. Safia told me I was crazy to come here and she was right."

I fought the frown that threatened to descend on my face. "Crazy? That's a bit harsh considering she left her whole life behind to move here."

"Yeah, but she wanted to. I like my life in the city—at least, I used to. Maybe if she came down and helped me sometimes, I wouldn't do stupid things like drive through a snowstorm to catch a break."

"*Attempt* to drive through a snowstorm," I corrected him. "You never got where you needed to be and the fact that you tried tells me how desperate you were."

"Raging, more like."

I wasn't about to argue with him over his state of mind. I

didn't know Rami as well as I wanted to, but the stubborn frown creasing his forehead told me all I needed to know about how he'd react to me telling him how I thought he felt. And his instinctive *go fuck yourself* would've been relatable. I didn't like being told how to feel. Why would he?

Why would anyone?

I found my boots at the back door and stamped into them, then stepped outside, bracing myself against the cold wind. The air was moist, as if rain was coming, and I didn't know how I felt about that. I liked this limbo I'd found myself in with Rami. I wasn't ready to give it up.

The thought of the snow thawing sunk a cloud over my mood. A deep, dark, melancholy that often sent me to the whisky bottle when I was on my own. I fought it, mind. I was good at that. Bad moods were annoying, and I didn't want to be annoyed while I still had Rami in my house. This was my wildest dreams come true—the PG ones, at least. I wasn't going to waste it sulking over the fact that, eventually, it would have to end.

I found the pie among the stack I'd bought to feed my crew when it was my turn to cook Sunday dinner up at the main house. My next go wasn't for a while yet, but I liked to be prepared. It meant circumstances like these didn't derail my sanity, and that I'd been forward-thinking enough to buy turkey and cranberry pies for my December slot. Go me.

The looming rain began to fall as I trudged back to the house, big fat drops that would dislodge some of the snow and leave treacherous ice behind. It wouldn't do much to rescue Rami's car, but Paddy McCann's truck would be okay. *He could be gone tomorrow.* Like, literally gone. He'd already admitted he'd made a mistake bringing Charlie up here. What if he got in Paddy's truck and went straight back home?

To Manchester? The place where I'd left a piece of myself on the grimy floor of a D wing cell?

I was not in the mood to relive that mess. I ignored the tremor in my hands and shoved the back door open. Rami was nowhere in sight and my heart clenched, but the tiny slippers at the bottom of the stairs calmed my raging pulse more than I could say. *You're a strange man, Hawthorne.*

Cooking dinner kept me occupied while Rami and Charlie were upstairs, and because I gave zero hoots about morphing into a carbon copy of my dad, I turned the radio on for company. It was late enough in the year that the playlists were rammed with cheesy Christmas songs and listeners calling in to rant about overcrowded shops. It was a world away from anything I cared about, but I listened anyway, grumbling under my breath when the first world problems hacked me off too much.

A low laugh from the doorway sounded a little while later, and I felt Rami's presence like warm water being trickled over my skin. "Talking to that pie, are ya?"

"I'm talking to Agnes, actually. She doesn't think anyone from further south than Blackburn should be up here."

"And you disagree with her?"

"Course I do. Tourists pay the bills. If they didn't fill the pub all summer long, there'd be nowhere to go for a pint in the winter."

"I always forget there's a community here."

"Easy to do from the top of the mountain. Safia doesn't come down much and at this time of year, only when the kids need stuff she doesn't trust me to buy for her."

"You do that?" Rami pushed off the doorframe he'd claimed as his leaning post while he was here. He ventured farther into the kitchen, then stopped as if he'd forgotten why. "Shop for my sister, I mean?"

"Sometimes. We're neighbours."

"You probably know her better than I do these days."

"Doubt it. Cheese-swapping and letting her kids run riot round my farm doesn't make me blood."

"Dude, they call you Uncle Fen."

I had nothing to counter with. I had no idea why the McCade kids had gifted me that privilege, and I hated the introspective frown it had put on Rami's face, but I liked the affection they shared with me. Their innocence had kept me alive at a time in my life when I'd struggled to breathe, and I loved them for that.

Rami stayed quiet while I heated the pie and opened a can of beans. Charlie was already in bed, so we ate together at the table. He cleaned up, and I drifted to the couch with a beer.

He followed sometime later, his own beer in hand. "It's nice to drink with someone," he said with a sigh. "I don't bother at home, cos I'm not sure I'd stop."

"Been there."

He cast me a curious glance. "When?"

The simple question caught me off guard. My hand rose to the scar on my neck, and Rami's sharp gaze caught it before I did.

His eyes widened.

I lowered my hand and gripped my beer bottle, bracing myself for the question, but baulked at the last minute and stood. "I'm empty. Back in a sec."

In the kitchen, I necked the beer I still had and opened the fridge despite knowing there were no more bottles in there and if I really wanted another I'd have to go to the garage. The bare shelf seemed to taunt me. Or maybe it was my subconscious telling me not to be such a tool. I was ninety percent sure Rami already knew I'd been shanked. Clamming up and running away every time it came up was ridiculous, and yet...I'd been doing it for more than a year and I didn't know how to stop. The deafening thud in my chest could be quieted by whisky, but the coward in my head never took a day off.

Don't be so hard on yourself. You nearly died. It's okay to be messed-up. But the spiel I'd spent a decade serenading traumatised offenders with didn't work on me.

Shame, because my inner monologue spoke nothing but truth.

A warm hand grazed my back, light fingertips that travelled from one side of my ribcage to the other. "Hey," Rami whispered.

"Hey." I didn't turn round.

Rami stepped closer, his breath feathering my bare skin as his scalding palm slid higher until it was splayed across the nape of my neck, his thumb millimetres from the scar I'd fled the room to avoid thinking about. He pressed tight against me, his body fitting to mine, and wound his other arm around my abdomen.

It was a hug, of sorts, but it felt like an intervention too. A hot intervention, if there was such a thing, because my head could be as noisy and scratchy as it wanted, there was nothing in the world loud enough to drown out the effect Rami's touch had on the heat of my blood. The speed at which it pumped around my body, pooling south with a heady kick to my thundering pulse.

I let out a slow, shaky breath. "What are you doing to me, Stone?"

Rami laughed, soft and warm. "You looked lost, so I found you."

"Lost? In my own house?"

"Hey, it's my interpretation, not fact. We can debate it if you like, or..."

"Or what?"

"Or you can come back to the couch and drink my beer while we watch *Die Hard*. It's my favourite Christmas film."

"It's not a Christmas film."

"Okay, well...you're wrong, but whatever. Come sit so we can argue about it."

I didn't want to argue with him, but the rest of his proposition sounded like heaven.

The fridge door slipped from my hand, swinging shut. I turned around. Rami smiled and took my hand, leading me back to the sofa I rarely got round to sitting on when I was alone. It was low-slung and comfortable, the kind of couch that sucked you in and spat you out again eight hours later with cushion imprints on your cheek and drool on your chin.

It was built for two.

Rami sat, tugging me along with him. I was a stone heavier than him, but there was zero fight in me as he pulled me down next to him.

He passed me his beer.

I took it and pressed the bottle to my lips, seeking perspective in the cool glass.

None came. Rami turned the volume up on the TV. Bruce Willis filled the screen without a festive light or bauble to be seen. Smirking, I drained the beer and sank into the couch, heaviness smothering me, but not the bad kind.

Rami chuckled and plucked the empty bottle from my fingers.

He put it somewhere—I missed the details—and somehow I found myself leaning on him, sliding down his hard, warm body until my head was pillowed on his belly.

And then, because this strange limbo we were trapped in persisted in warped moments of perfection, I fell asleep.

5

Rami

Paddy came for me at the crack of dawn, startling me out of the deep sleep I'd sunk into on Fen's sofa before anyone, even Charlie, was awake.

He let himself in the front door, calling my name, and giving Fen just enough time to scramble from my lap and disappear.

Head thick, I staggered upright as my favourite—and only—brother-in-law filled the kitchen doorway, big and brawny in a way that made Fen seem small. "There you are." His bright gaze found me. "I told your sister you'd be dead to the world, but she wanted me to come as soon as the road cleared."

"It's cleared?" I cast a mystified glance to the window. The ground was still white, but the overnight rain had flattened it and the morning sun was sparkling bright, glittering off the frosted trees.

"Kind of," Paddy clarified. "It's still icy as hell, but the tyres on my truck can handle it now it's not a foot deep."

I opened my mouth again, but nothing came out. My phone was on the arm of the couch, half hidden by the blanket I'd pulled over Fen when he'd fallen asleep. I picked it up. It was 7 a.m., the witching hour for me, but practically lunchtime for Paddy.

What about Fen? What time does he usually get up?

It was almost painful how much I wanted to know, but a comical yawn from the top of the stairs pierced the air just as the alarm I'd set on my phone to wake before Charlie went off.

The obnoxious beeping hurt my brain. I shut it off and hurried to the foot of the stairs, catching Charlie as he reached the bottom, and swinging him onto my hip. "Mornin'. Guess who's here to see us?"

Charlie rubbed his nose. Stole mine and ate it, chewing as his tiny brain dropped into deep thought. "Fenny?"

"No, Fen lives here. This is his house. Who else did I tell you we'd be seeing while we were on Christmas Mountain?"

Charlie made a sound that could've been deciphered as Aunt Safia.

I gestured for him to try again. "Nearly. Who else?"
"Padda?"

Close enough. I grinned and turned so he could see the hulking bulk of his other favourite uncle loitering behind him. They'd only met a handful of times since Charlie had been born, but perhaps knowing this day would come, I'd bombarded Charlie with photos and videos of the family we shared. Face-timed whenever Safia's patchy Internet signal had allowed. In the absence of in-person contact, I'd built Paddy up to be the BFG's friendliest friend.

I hadn't lied.

He bore down on us and stole Charlie from my arms with his massive hands. Charlie's eyes widened to that terrifying precipice where he was either going to scream in terror or shriek with sheer joy. Most times it was eighty-twenty in favour of terror, especially with strangers. Sweet Fen seemed to be the exception, and with Paddy, my photo scrolling on the iPad in favour of bedtime stories had paid off.

Charlie laughed as if Paddy was the funniest thing he'd ever seen and wrapped his arms around his neck. "Padda!"

"That's Uncle Padda to you," Paddy grumped, "but whatever. Where's all your stuff, little man? Are you ready to take a ride in my big truck?"

Truck was the magic word where Charlie was concerned. Paddy set him down, and he scampered around Fen's house, collecting the handful of things we'd brought with us and stuffing them into his bag.

I was wearing one of Fen's flannel shirts. It was too big, but it was warm, and smelled of him, and there wasn't a single part of me that considered taking it off.

Charlie's bag was full. He handed it to Paddy who peered inside, frowning. "This is all you brought? Where's Uncle Rama's stuff?"

"Diden bring none."

"Any," I corrected, avoiding Paddy's gaze as I searched around for the few things I had brought—my phone, my shoes, my optimistic city-boy coat.

I realised too late I was clutching my phone already. Scowling, I shoved it into my pocket and finally approached Paddy to embrace him. His large arms crushed me, and I welcomed the oblivion, but at the same time, the sensation that they were the wrong fucking arms made me cut the hug short and push back, searching for Fen with little conscious thought.

He was nowhere in sight. He'd vanished into thin air and only the empty beer bottle on the floor by the couch convinced me the night we'd spent together hadn't been a baked bean-induced hallucination.

Christ, you're ridiculous.

Yup. I really was. Maybe the mountain air was getting to me, because as much as I'd thought about Fen back in the city, it hadn't affected my ability to string a coherent thought together.

All the more reason to go home.

I shrugged into my coat and did a last scan of the space around us for mess and toddler detritus, but came up blank. The toddler in question had done a good job at erasing our brief disruption to Fen's life and I wasn't sure how I felt about that.

Actually, I wasn't sure how I felt about anything, save the fact I was still half asleep.

Paddy took pity on me and commandeered Charlie into his shoes and his Spiderman coat. He took him and the bag out to the truck while I trailed behind, still searching for Fen. For a big man, he was apparently an expert at making himself invisible. Or maybe I just didn't know him well enough to have a fucking clue where he might've gone. It wasn't as if I had any idea how he spent his days and nights when he wasn't rescuing me from my bonehead life choices.

We reached the truck. Paddy had every car seat under the sun strapped to the backseat and he hoisted Charlie into the correct one without the pedantic instructions Damon and Leanne had always needed. *He's a good dad. The best. Maybe Charlie would—*

"Not sneaking off, are you?"

I spun around.

Fen was behind me, dress code: level ten lumberjack, and the sight of him went straight to my dick.

See? You're not even close to parent material.

I shook my head, praying the warmth in my blood didn't show in my face. "I didn't know where you went."

"Work," Fen said as if he hadn't been passed out on top of me ten minutes ago. "There's a lot to do now the road is moving, though I'm not sure it's safe to head south just yet." He fixed Paddy with a stare that almost scared me. "You're not going that way, are you?"

"Nope. Safia wants to roast Uncle Rama before he gets to go home. I reckon she'll be done in five to seven business days."

Great. I refrained from rolling my eyes like a petulant child and gave Fen my full attention while Paddy got in the truck. "Looks like I'm not going too far just yet."

Fen grunted, his slightly bloodshot eyes giving away that perhaps he was feeling as shambolic as I was. "Far enough."

"Is it?"

"Yeah. I don't like the look of that road."

"Paddy wouldn't drive Charlie if he didn't think it was safe."

That earned me another grunt, and a pouty bottom lip that would've been adorable without the storm raging in Fen's cobalt gaze.

I frowned and took a subtle sidestep to the back of the truck where Paddy couldn't see me. "What's wrong?"

"Hmm?"

I reached for Fen and discovered his hip, my fingers somehow finding their way beneath his winter clothes to find bare skin. It was another fortunate accident, and something else I didn't regret despite the complication of craving so much more. *Focus on Charlie. It's why you're here.*

True, but even a soul as cynical as mine had to believe fate had dumped me in Fen's snowy driveway for a reason.

I rubbed his skin again, ignoring the buzz of electricity that zapped my veins. "Talk to me. I'll listen."

Fen's smile was faint and sad. "You don't need to do that. Just…"

"What?"

"Don't leave without saying goodbye, okay? I don't want to do it that way again."

I didn't want to do it at all. I wanted to transplant our lives back to a place where we'd been two simple men working in the same building, flirting over stale biscuits and release plans for offenders who deserved another chance. But at the same time, this mountain was Fen's home; his past, his present, and his future. He belonged here and the goodbye that sounded so fucking wrong was inevitable. "I won't leave like that, I promise."

"So I'll see you again?"

"Yeah. Lucky you, eh?"

"I'd say so." Fen's smile finally deepened enough to seem real. He stared at my lips, then pulled back with an infinitesimal shake of his head. "Take care, Stone."

"You too. And Fen?"

"Yeah?"

"Thanks for watching my favourite Christmas film with me."

I gave him a saccharine smile and climbed into the truck, and I didn't have to look back to see his answering grin.

It was imprinted on my heart already.

"That's the stupidest thing I've ever heard."

I closed my eyes, resisting the temptation to press my thumbs into the sockets, remembering in one fell swoop why conversations with my forthright sister stressed me the fuck out. "It's not stupid. It could work if we wanted it to."

Safia banged a cast iron pot on her huge kitchen table. I was sitting on a chair made of wood from Fen's forest.

Fen's forest. Wow. It sounded like bad aftershave.

Or a picture-perfect life that didn't involve me.

"It won't work," Safia snapped. "You can't be a full-time parent, hold down your ridiculous job, and have a life of your own. It's not fair."

"I know. That's why I'm saying you could have Charlie for the holidays—when he starts school, I mean. And he can go to nursery while I work."

"You want to put him in full-time nursery care?"

"Part-time."

"What about your mortgage? And your student loans? And everything else you'd have to pay on a part-time salary?"

"I'll manage. I got this far."

"Only because you took a mortgage holiday and a partial sabbatical from your job."

"No, because I know how to count my own money. I'm not a fucking child."

Safia didn't flinch. She sat and ladled me a bowl of the casserole she'd dished out for lunch. She pushed it across the table, but I ignored it, appetite MIA since our tense conversation had escalated into a full-blown Stone family drama.

Paddy had taken all the kids to feed the goats, Charlie

safely tied to his back so he wouldn't trip on the uneven muddy ground that was a world away from the concrete and pollution he was used to.

"Look," Safia tried again, softer this time, without the edge that wound me the fuck up. "I just don't think it's sustainable for you to work yourself into the ground thirty-nine weeks of the year, then dump him up here for the rest of it—"

"Dump?"

"Bad word choice. That's not what I mean."

"What do you mean, then?"

"I mean if that's how things go, all you get from raising Charlie is the hard stuff. The school runs, the bills, the horrible bedtimes when the little bastards won't sleep and you have to go to work in the morning. You're gifting the magical moments to me and it's not fair, Rama, to either of you, but most of all you."

"I'd be fine, Saf. Honest."

"I don't want you to be fine. I want you to be happy."

I snorted, scrubbing a hand down my face. "You think I'm not happy?"

"I think you're a mess."

"Nice."

"Deny it then. Let's keep fighting instead of enjoying the fact that you're up here with us for the first time in a fucking eternity."

"Has it been that long?"

"Of course it has. You never left the city after Charlie was born. You didn't trust Damon not to drop him in the bath."

She wasn't even joking. I'd been in Charlie's life from the moment Damon and Leanne had brought him home from the hospital, because the sad reality was he'd needed me to be. And then just when I'd thought Damon was going to turn it around, he'd died.

I hadn't come up for air since. Safia's kitchen felt almost as surreal as Fen's had, and my hands shook around the nuclear mug of coffee she'd presented me with a while ago. It was still warm, but I was scared to drink it. "I spoke to Elaine yesterday."

"The social worker?"

I nodded. "She thinks custody is a foregone conclusion. I was the only one pushing for Leanne to be in Charlie's life. The team supporting us thought she'd have done a bunk months ago."

"She might come back," Safia said darkly. "When she needs cash and wants the benefit payments."

"It won't matter if I have custody. She'd have to take me to court to get him back and she's never going to do that."

"Won't stop her making your life miserable, like she did Damon's."

"That was different. Damon had already made his bed. All she did was push him into it. And if she did start trouble on the street, I'd just move."

"How, though? If you're on a part-time wage, how are you going to raise the money you'd need to sell your flat and buy another one somewhere else? You already told me you're tied into a fixed-rate mortgage with early settlement fees."

Why? Why the hell did I ever tell her that? "I don't know. I might not have to."

"He'd have a better life up here. You both would."

"You keep him then!" My frustration finally overwhelmed me and my shout rang out in the big kitchen, reverberating off the shaker cabinets and flagstone tiles. "It's not like I don't know he'd be better off with you."

"Oh for God's sake." Safi rolled her eyes to the ceiling before fixing me with her best glare again. "You don't get it, do you? It's not *me* that would make his life up here worth living, it's *you,* Rama. It always has been. That kid loves you like you're his biological father and *that's* why you need to have something better than the bullshit you've come up here with."

"So what's your solution then? Unless you're volunteering to give up your fucking life and move to Manchester to help me out?"

"The solution is obvious." Safia somehow laced her acid tone with love. "You need to go home, pack your shit up, and come back here for good."

It was my turn to roll my eyes at the full circle our conversation had taken in the two hours we'd been having it. To Safia, it was that simple: abandon my entire existence and come and live hers, but whichever way I looked at it I couldn't see myself milking goats and building fences for the rest of my life, all the while trying to play parent and teacher to Charlie when whatever Safia thought, she was so much fucking better at it. And how would I work? On top of offender rehabilitation, I was a qualified counsellor, but with no reliable Internet coverage, I couldn't even work remotely.

We flogged the same horse all afternoon. Eventually, Safia bullied me into agreeing I'd stick around for a few days and rest while she helped me with Charlie. "You're worn out, Ram. It's no wonder you can't see sense."

I gave her a subtle finger. She caught me, but she was as tired of fighting as I was, and she brought out the cake as a peace offering. "So..." She handed me a slice of spice-laden fruit cake. "How do you know Fen? I couldn't make sense of what you told me on the phone. The line was so bad."

"From the prison. He was an officer there before he came back here. We worked on some cases together."

Safia's eyes widened a touch. "In Manchester?"

"That's where I live," I snapped before I caught myself. I had no desire to reignite the festering row between us. "I mean, yeah. HMP Manchester. He was personal officer to some of the offenders I took on from there. We got on well, and apparently we still do, though it shocked the shit out of me to see him again. I never saw him after..." I trailed off, all but certain Safia knew nothing about the circumstances that had brought Fen back to Christmas Mountain.

"After what?"

"After he left. I disappeared for a while after Damon died. When I got back to the prison, he was gone."

Safia drummed her fingers on the thick butcher's block table, gaze more speculative than I could stand right now. Was I that transparent? Could she already see my fixation with Fen growing fresh roots? "You know," she said. "It was strange when he came back here. When we bought the land from his dad, their plan was always to rent that cottage out as a holiday home and sell the log farm when Isaac died. I didn't know Fen was here until a month after he showed up—it was almost like he'd come to hide away from the world."

"And now?"

Safia shrugged. "Life moves on, doesn't it? He runs the farm himself and makes my kids laugh like they aren't little devils incarnate. He's the best friend we have around here, I just wish he let us be the same to him."

"He doesn't let you?"

"Not even a little bit. When he comes up here, he'll stick around sometimes to eat with us, but he won't hang out late or spend the night in the cabin. I thought it was because he didn't want the memories of his own childhood around him so much, then he told me he never spent much time up here, so…" She spread her hands. "I don't know. He's such a nice man, I hate the thought of him being lonely."

"He is a nice man," I agreed. How could I not?

"Gorgeous too," Safia inserted slyly.

I scowled. "What does that have to do with anything?"

"Nothing. Just saying."

"Well, don't. He's been through enough without—" I clamped my mouth shut, but it was too late. My runaway tongue had betrayed Fen and Safia's eyebrows had disappeared into her thick, dark hair. "Never mind."

"Clearly, you *do* mind," she said. "What do you know about Fen that I don't?"

"Nothing."

"Sure about that?"

"Sure as houses, mate. I don't know anything about him other than how he takes his tea."

And even that knowledge was shaky. The Fen I'd known in Manchester hadn't had a sweet tooth, but the lumbersexual version tipped two spoons of sugar into his tea mug.

"I don't believe you," Safia said. "He's a different man to the one who came up here five years ago to help his dad clear our land before the sale went through, and I've always wondered why."

"Maybe it's none of your business."

"It's not my business in the slightest, doesn't stop me thinking about it. We love Fen. He's part of our family when he lets us make the fuss of him he deserves, and I hate to think that he's ever suffered alone because I didn't know he needed us."

I felt bad then. My sister was the fiercest supporter any

soul could ever wish for. I was lucky to have her, and so was Fen, in whatever capacity their friendship had formed in the years I'd been absent and/or oblivious. "Look, there's a reason he left his job at the prison and came back here, but I don't know the details, and he doesn't seem to want to talk about it, so maybe it's best we both leave it well alone, eh?"

Safia let it go, but as the conversation returned to Charlie's future, I found myself stuck on Fen. Something had changed in him since I'd found him staring into the fridge last night. Or perhaps it hadn't and all that had happened was he'd forgotten to lock the gates on whatever went on behind his pretty eyes.

Regardless, he was as mysterious as he was open and warm, and wasn't that an addictive puzzle? Compelling enough to consume every thought that wasn't about Charlie, though that wasn't new.

What *was* new was the captive audience I found myself with every moment I wasn't taking a piss. Charlie. Addie. Mae. All three of them attached themselves to me like Velcro, and it was early evening by the time Safia took pity on me and hustled them all away for a bath in the "pig shed".

No joke. My sister's shower rooms were powered by solar panels, but she had an old copper tub in a barn that was heated by a pellet stove. It was kind of luxurious if you didn't mind the smell of the nearby sow and their piglets.

I did mind, so I stayed where I was on the couch, nursing the mulled cider Paddy had brought me and picking at a plate of nutmeg-spiced biscuits. My phone was on the arm of the couch, lit up with work emails I'd have to spend the next morning answering. There was a voicemail too, from Charlie's social worker, thanking me for keeping her updated. I appreciated the sentiment. How many times had I sat waiting for an offender who had already been recalled to prison and no fucker had bothered to tell me?

Too many.

Still, her trust in me was scary. I didn't want autonomy. I wanted someone to make the hard decisions for me. *Go home. Back to your real life.*

Instead, I cleared the email notifications from my lock screen and stared into my sister's fireplace. It was more rustic than Fen's—no stove or guard, just a hole in the wall housing a glowing pile of burning logs, timber that had come from Fen's land, no doubt. Thinking about him was the welcome distraction it had always been, but as hard as I tried to focus on his rugged, unshaven jaw, his broad shoulders, and deep, masculine voice, the more my brain seemed stuck on the frown creasing his brow as he'd slept in my arms, and the sadness in his gaze when I'd left him that morning.

The lights on Safia's Christmas tree came on. They were multi-coloured, and half obscured by the sheer volume of decorations, but the dancing light still reminded me of Fen, and I let my imagination run wild, picturing him felling the enormous tree that took up most of Safia's living room. Hoisting it onto his broad shoulders and onto Paddy's truck, his blue eyes sparkling in the winter sunlight. *God, why does he have to be so fucking beautiful? I have real shit to worry about.*

Something warm landed on my chest. I glanced down to see a bundle of pale skin, tiny limbs, and enormous brown eyes. Lalla, my youngest niece.

Paddy sank onto the couch beside me. "Don't worry, she's a quiet one."

I adjusted the baby to where Charlie had spent most of his early months, sprawled on my left arm while I'd typed on my laptop with my free hand. My supervisor back then had told me I looked *"fraught"* on the days I'd actually made it to work. I'd figured him for a bit of a cunt, but hindsight was a wonderful thing. "I never minded the screaming. It let me know I hadn't fucked up enough to kill him."

Paddy snorted. "As if. You're an amazing dad."

"I'm not his dad, though, am I?"

"Might as well be now. Damon gave it a good go for a while there, but it was always going to end up here. You know, that, right?"

I sighed. "Maybe."

Paddy didn't argue with me. It wasn't his way, and living with Safia, he was well-versed in the reality that there was little point. Stones were stubborn. We couldn't be told and we had to learn every lesson the hard way. "Hold still," he said instead.

He held his phone up and snapped a selfie of us on the couch with Lalla.

I gave him the finger. "What did you do that for?"

"Two reasons. First, to prove you were actually here when you disappear down south again. Second, I'm sending it to Fen. He asked me how you were doing and I hate typing on my phone. A picture speaks a thousand words, eh?"

I watched him fire the photo into the ether, torn between calling him a nasty word he didn't deserve and snatching the phone out of his hand to get Fen's number. Considering the sweet-scented bundle on my chest, neither seemed appropriate, so I settled for glaring at him until he noticed.

Then glaring some more when he didn't give a shit. "I'd rather have sent him a thank-you text than a picture of me slumming it on your couch in your donkey-sized clothes."

"Text him then."

"I don't have his number."

"Why not? Thought you were old friends?"

"Not quite. We worked together once upon a time." I kept it vague. If Safia hadn't filled Paddy in, that was his problem. "I guess we are friends, though. Maybe."

Okay. I was getting less vague. And Paddy possessed a penetrating stare Safia's terminal impatience denied her. He needled me with it, silent and searing. Then wordlessly picked up my phone, typing in Charlie's birthday to unlock it. He loaded Fen's number into my contacts and opened the messaging app. "Just so happens we're sitting in the hot spot for phone signal, and the spare room is the other, by the window. What do you want to say? I'll type it out for you."

"Thought you hated typing on phones?"

"I do, but I'll make an exception for you, brother."

Paddy wasn't my brother, but I'd often wished Damon had been like him—kind, strong, hardworking. Annoying in ways that didn't set my entire life on fire. "Just tell him...uh, just say thanks for the hospitality. I appreciate it, and...fuck, I don't know."

"That'll do." Paddy thumbed out the message and hit send before I could catch a glimpse of the words he'd typed.

He passed the phone back with a cheeky grin and when I scanned the screen, I saw why.

Rami: *Thanks for the hospitality. I owe you one. Collect your debt whenever you like x*

Git. In my head, I curled my hand into a fist and punched Paddy's massive bicep as hard as I could. But when I reached for the anger, it wasn't there.

After all, he'd only written what I would have if I hadn't been stuck on a loop of introspection. And the kiss at the end?

Wishful thinking, because *fuck* I wished I'd kissed him

goodbye. Even if I never saw him again, at least I'd know if his lips were as soft as they looked, and pondering on that kept me occupied for the rest of the evening.

It was late by the time I relinquished Lalla and drifted across my sister's yard to the log cabin she called the spare room. Charlie was sleeping with Addie in the main house, gifting me a welcome respite from parental night duty, and I couldn't deny the cabin was everything I'd dreamed of when I'd paced my city centre flat with a pissed-off baby in my arms. Warm, secluded, and darker than hell once I'd turned the lamp off, it was fucking heaven.

I plugged my phone into the socket built into the wall. Buoyed by the knowledge that signal was shite up here, I'd resisted checking it every ten seconds for a response to the Paddy-fuelled message I'd sent Fen, but the blank screen now was still a kick in the dick I didn't need.

Twat.

Me. Not him. I ditched my phone on the dresser, stripped off my borrowed clothes, and crawled, naked, into the timber bed. The sheets were cool against my skin, and smelled of woodsmoke and...Fen. *Wow. You're obsessed, mate.* Damnit. How had that happened? I'd been hot for him since we'd met, but I wasn't a dude who nurtured attachments. When it came to matters of the heart, I was a lone wolf. Always had been. Grindr was my best friend when I had the time. When I didn't, I was happy alone.

But...I wasn't happy now. The unanswered text festered in my mind, and despite the brain-aching fatigue smothering me, I couldn't sleep.

I was wide awake when my phone flashed at 2 a.m.

Probably an email. Ignore it.

I got up and padded across the cabin, the chilled air

biting into my bare skin with a discomfort that was somehow stimulating. Or maybe my cock was as much of a weirdo as I was. Either way, I was semi-hard for no reason whatsoever.

My phone was still flashing. I picked it up, expecting disappointment.

A rush hit my heart, hard and fast, and yeah...maybe my cock too.

Fen: *I'll find you x*

Rami: *I'll wait x*

Fen

Two days. That was how long it took me before I invented a fictitious reason to drive my Land Rover up the mountain to check on Rami. Knowing he was still there and that he wanted to see me had settled the dancing nerves in my heart while I'd tried to figure out a rational-sounding explanation for appearing unannounced at Safia's place, but my pulse still pounded in my ears as the homestead came into view.

I'd brought firewood, despite the fact I'd helped Paddy stack his log store two weeks ago with enough to last him till spring, a reality he somehow managed to ignore as he waved me through the gate and glanced at my loaded back seat.

He opened the door and hoisted the unnecessary sacks onto his Hulk-esque shoulders. "Rami's up the barns," he said. "Loving life, no doubt."

"Is that sarcasm?"

"Who? Me?" Paddy's grin was wicked. "Never."

I thought back to that faraway world that had existed before I'd snoozed the night away in Rami's lap. The one where Rami had told me in no uncertain terms how the life Paddy and I shared wasn't one he could ever see himself living. *"...don't know if you've noticed, but I'm not a man-of-the-mountain kind of bloke."*

Fair enough. But when I poked my head into the barn that had once housed my grandfather's Highland cattle, I begged to differ. Wearing clothes I was pretty sure belonged to Safia, Rami was bottle-feeding a piglet with one hand, while hammering a nail into a broken trough with the other. With Charlie hanging off his back and the other kids at his feet, he seemed perfectly at home, and *damn* if he didn't look like all the man-of-the-mountain I'd ever need.

Easy. I shook my head, grateful no one had noticed me yet, but the moment I had to collect myself while I drank Rami in was brief. A fleeting moment of heat and warmth so intense it took my breath away.

Then Addie saw me. His face lit up and he came screaming across the barn with Mae hot on his heels.

The commotion startled Charlie. He tightened his arms around Rami's neck, jumping out of his tiny skin. Rami dropped the hammer. It hit his foot and he cursed, loudly, in his glorious gravel-toned voice. "Fucking mother*fucker!*"

Snorting, I caught Addie before he barrelled into me, hooking one arm around his waist and the other around Mae's, swinging them both over my shoulders the way their dad had with the superfluous firewood.

Their laughter was life. I spun around, making them—and myself—dizzy. I'd brought with me a soul-deep craving to set eyes on Rami, but I loved these kids. And for reasons I didn't quite understand, they loved me too.

I brought them both upright, hugging them tight for a moment before I set Addie down. Mae was a snuggler—once she was attached to me, she liked to stay that way until she got a better offer.

Today, though, she squirmed to get down and slotted her tiny hand in mine. "Come see, come see. Uncle Rama and Charlie."

She tugged me into the barn and presented Rami and Charlie to me as if I'd never seen them before, pulling them forward, one by one.

Charlie giggled and pointed at me. "Fenny!"

Rami?

Yeah. His smirk was everything I'd driven up here to see.

Wide and droll.

Dirty.

"Pleased to meet you," he said dryly.

"Back atcha. Nice clothes."

He laughed. "Guess I'm lucky my sister dresses like you."

"My shirt looks better on you than it does on me."

"I disagree."

"Do you?"

"Yup."

Rami grinned, but as gorgeous as he was when he smiled, the stress lines he'd brought up the mountain were still there, though he didn't seem as monumentally knackered.

I bent and scooped Charlie from the floor, fitting him to my hip. He gave me a toothy smile. I pulled a piece of straw from his hair, then turned my attention back to Rami. "How's things?"

"All right."

"Really?"

Rami's smile waned a touch. He ruffled Charlie's hair,

then grabbed Mae from his feet as if he didn't quite know what to do with himself while I'd claimed Charlie. "Things are complicated. Safia thinks I should quit my entire life and move up here, and I think she's bonkers."

"Why?"

Rami rolled his eyes. "She's bonkers for lots of reasons, but...fuck, I can't live like this, you know? I've only been here a few days and I already can't deal with having someone in my face every two seconds, even faces I like."

He tweaked Mae's nose. She responded by thwacking her palm against his cheek.

Addie objected, jumping up and pulling her long hair.

Her shriek was deafening.

Rami sighed and clamped a gentle hand over her mouth. "Wow. Do you have hot air balloons for lungs?"

His hand swallowed Mae's answer. She frowned deeply, but she'd met her match where it came to heavy scowling. Rami wasn't like me. He was unswayed by her fury and lacked the compulsive need to make her happy.

She wriggled until he put her down.

Then she punched Addie and ran off.

It was his turn to screech, but I caught him before it stretched out into the kind of bloodcurdling wail Rami clearly didn't have the patience for.

Somehow in the year or so, I'd turned into my grandad and had a pocket full of sweets. I gave Addie a Fruitella and pressed my finger to his lips. "Don't tell your sister. Or your mum for that matter."

"What about my dad?"

"Sure, you can tell him. He'd never snitch on me."

"Because you'll tell her he got drunk and took all his clothes off at the pub?"

"Something like that."

Addie laughed and ran off, disappearing with Mae into the great outdoors they called home. I felt their freedom as though it was my own and I couldn't fathom why Rami didn't want it, for himself or for Charlie, but I kept it to myself. After all, it wasn't as if I hadn't spent my entire adolescence wishing I was somewhere else. *Took fifteen damn years to learn how wrong you were.*

Fifteen years and a shank to my throat.

I shivered.

Rami eyed me. "Someone walk over your grave?"

How he knew I wasn't just cold, I had no idea.

I also had no desire to elaborate, so I turned away from the question and took Charlie outside.

He followed and, like magic, Safia appeared and plucked Charlie from my arms. "Snack time, little man. You boys want anything?"

I shook my head.

Rami did too. "You fed me, like, ten minutes ago. I don't need to eat again until next Tuesday."

"Don't be a git."

"Leave me alone then."

Safia muttered a horrendous insult under her breath and whisked Charlie inside.

Rami snorted and made no move to follow her. "Man, I love her, but give me fucking strength."

"You don't think that's what she's trying to do?"

"I don't need eight meals a day."

"You might if you lived up here. It's hard graft, especially in winter."

"I don't live up here."

His tone was even, but the words were clipped as they

registered in my brain, and I found myself irritated that he seemed to think it would be the worst thing in the world if things were different. Or maybe I was defensive. After all, it wasn't just Safia's life he was dismissing. It was my family's entire history.

But the spike in my blood didn't last long. Rami was tired, in more ways than one. And *his* life was closing in on him. My sensitivities weren't important. "I'm sorry it's tough for you up here. I guess I'd kind of assumed it would be better with your people around you."

"It is better. It's just—fuck, I'm sorry. I'm just a moody bastard and I'm pissed off with myself."

"Why?"

He shrugged, and the gesture seemed so helpless that I put my hands on his shoulders as if it was the most natural and normal thing in the world. As if we hadn't spent eighteen long months apart with nothing but dead silence between us.

"Hey." I gave him a gentle squeeze. "You want to escape for a few hours later?"

"Escape?"

"I'm heading into town to check up on our pop-up shop in the village. If you came with me, we could get a pint after? Maybe have that date we missed out on back in Manchester?"

A spark flared in Rami's dark gaze, overshadowing the stress that had clouded his expression before. "You realise you never actually asked me out, right? So I never said yes."

"You would've done, though."

"Oh yeah?"

"Yeah." I knew he would've. And I knew how it would've gone down too. I'd have taken him to the ale bar on the corner just before the madness of Canal Street began. We'd have sunk three pints of whatever looked good, then gone for a walk, hand-in-hand, before I'd kissed him beneath a streetlight, our skin damp from the light spring rain.

I squeezed him again. "Tell me I'm wrong."

Rami closed his eyes. "I can't."

"Why not?"

"Because I would've said yes."

"And then what?"

Rami opened his eyes and fixed me with his dirtiest grin. "And then I guess we'd never have looked at each other in the same way again."

Okay, so he clearly had a different idea of how first dates went down and I was willing to compromise.

So willing, as long as it made him smile like that. "Say yes now. I know everything is different and complicated, but we're still the same people."

"Are we?" Rami covered my hands with his and his gaze turned complex again. "How can that be true when so much has happened to both of us?"

He had me there, and I didn't have an answer that wasn't knee-deep in emotions I spent most of my life these days trying to avoid.

I nodded slowly and hung my head. "You're right."

"About what?"

"All of it, I just—"

"What?"

I forced my head up again, noticing for the first time that someone had drawn a rudimentary snowman on his neck. It looked a hell of a lot better than the puncture scar on mine, and I laughed.

Rami frowned. "What's so funny?"

"This." I rubbed at it with my thumb. "Addie, right? He's always got a Sharpie in his pocket."

"A *permanent* Sharpie."

I winced.

Rami shook his head. "These fucking kids are feral. I'm pretty sure Charlie will have grown fangs by the time we go home."

"And when's that?"

"The weekend, maybe? I need to speak to my boss, but the signal is so bad up here, and Safia's Internet is awful, and…shit, sorry, you don't need to hear me rant."

"I don't mind."

"Well, I do. I want you to look at me and see the dude you wanted to date, not an angry yuppie trapped up a mountain."

"You're not a yuppie. For starters, you're not posh enough, and I hate to say it, but I think you're too old to qualify."

"I never pegged you for a pedantic twat."

"You never pegged me at all." Too late, I realised how filthy it sounded. Then Rami's rich, dirty laugh rang out and I had no regrets.

"Well, if I'm on a promise," he said. "Maybe I'll take you up on that date after all."

"Just want me for my body, Stone?"

He shrugged. "There's no *just* about you, Hawthorne."

I liked it better when he called me Fen, but the sentiment made my chest feel warm. "That's sweet. Listen, I've got to go, but I'm heading into town around three. Come down if you want to join me. If not…I'll see you around, okay? Maybe. If you don't leave without saying goodbye."

"I'd never do that."

"No?"

Rami slid his hands off mine and gripped my wrists, yanking me closer to him with a sudden strength that made me stumble. "*No,*" he whispered. "One way or another, you're stuck with me, I just...I don't know how much of me I have left to give yet."

He was so close I could've kissed him.

I settled for blurting out words with little conscious thought. "So don't give me anything. Just *be*, and come find me when you're ready."

▲

Rami

Of course I went to find him, propelled down the mountain, as if I needed any encouragement, by Safia's foot up my arse. "*We're making popcorn, watching* Elf, *and going to bed early, Charlie included. Stay out all night if you want.*"

She'd waggled her eyebrows.

I'd scowled so hard I'd nearly given myself a stroke, and yet here I was, hiking in the wind with a condom in my wallet.

Not that I'd put it there any time in recently. Lord knew how long it had been there, but still, I couldn't deny that the prospect of a date with Fen ending on a promise had my blood running so hot I barely felt the bitter winter wind as it blasted my face.

The mile-long hike passed quicker than I was prepared for too. Before I knew it, I was at Fen's gate, heart pummelling my ribcage, searching the horizon for any sign of his glorious shoulders.

All I got for my trouble was the beauty of the land where he lived. Thanks to the winter sun the snow had almost melted, leaving behind the lush green of the forest trees that covered Fen's side of Christmas Mountain. His house was nestled amongst them like a picture book, but as pretty as it was, I was craving a different kind of beautiful.

I vaulted the gate, glad my trainers had survived the great blizzard. Paddy had feet the size of canoes and I hadn't fancied rocking up to a date wearing Safia's lilac wellies.

The ground was still wet. My Adidas squelched in the grass as I approached Fen's house, then it occurred to me that he might not be there. His work day took him to the other side of the mountain, to the timber farm that had been in his family for generations, a route he'd walked when I'd been here last, but with his Land Rover nowhere in sight, I wondered if he'd driven.

Then I wondered if he'd left without me. Was I late?

I pulled out my phone to check.

Dropped it, obviously, because I was an absolute lad.

Cursing, I crouched to retrieve it. A low chuckle sounded behind me, and heat flooded me before I registered it was Fen, as if there was a deeper part of me that recognised him as something special.

As if I needed the reminder.

I rose and turned to face him. He was closer than I anticipated. More gorgeous too, if such a thing was possible. As I watched the slow smile cross his face, I decided it was. Also, that the lumberjack beard was a look he could keep forever, not that I'd been on the fence about it before. *And not that you'll be around to appreciate it forever, either. You don't live here, remember?*

Semantics.

Fen tilted his head, eyes sparkling. "You came."

"I did. Thought you'd gone without me when I couldn't see the car, though."

"Your car or mine?"

Damn. To tell the truth, I'd forgotten my car existed. "Um. Yours? I think?"

Fen laughed. "You didn't notice yours wasn't there, did you?"

"Nope. Where's it gone? Did it get eaten by wolves?"

"Towed, actually. Up to the barn. One of my blokes is a mechanic. He reckons he can fix it in a day once the part arrives."

"Works for me."

"Good. Because I put the part on Paddy's account."

"Lord. Really?"

"No. We got it cheap off eBay."

"Even better. You think it'll be done by Sunday?"

"Maybe." Something flickered in Fen's bright gaze. "You have somewhere to be?"

"Home," I said around a sigh. "I have to get back to work."

"What about Charlie?"

"What about him?"

Fen opened his mouth, then seemed to change his mind. "You know what? We don't need to have this conversation right now, out here, in the cold. Let me get the car and we can forget all about it for a while."

It was the best offer I'd had all year. The only thing I couldn't stomach was being separated from Fen for the three minutes it was going to take him to walk to the other side of his property to fetch his Land Rover.

So I went with him, taking in more of the landscape that I

hadn't seen while I'd been holed up in his house. "You've got your own Narnia."

Fen tracked my stare as it swept around the picturesque woodland, complete with a quaint rope swing. "Yeah, it's not bad. It's definitely a nicer place to wake up than where I was before."

"I'll bet. I can see a petrol station from my window back home."

"You don't ever get out of the city?"

"Not for fun. Closest I get is visiting Dante Pope at that stately home in Wilburn."

Fen's gaze flickered again. "He's still there?"

"They kept him on. Gave him a permanent position."

"With the lodgings too?"

I nodded. "I was worried about him for a while, but he's settled now. Happy, actually. Sometimes I forget what he was like when I met him."

Fen shuddered. "I don't. When I think about that place, I remember how scared he was, and how he didn't believe it would ever get better."

"But it did get better. Would you believe me if I told you his brother drives up every month to visit him?"

"No." We reached Fen's car. He opened the driver door and tilted his head as he frowned at me over the top of it. "He told me his brother hated him."

"Well, he doesn't now. I don't think they're exactly mates, but they're working harder at it than me and Damon ever did."

"Damon ever did, you mean."

I shrugged, gripping the handle of the passenger door, grounding myself in the cold metal against my palm. "Trust me, it wasn't all on him. I checked out for years before I realised he was sinking, and by then it was too late.”

“People sink or swim based on their own actions. You know that.”

“Do I?”

Fen snorted. “You’ve read the instruction manual. That counts, right?”

It counted for nothing in the end, but I hadn’t sought him out to bend his ear moaning. Damon was dead and I missed him, but I was literally on Christmas Mountain with the most gorgeous dude I’d ever known while my nephew lived his best life in any child’s paradise. In this moment, I didn’t have much to complain about.

We got into the car. Fen threw his arm around the back of my seat and reversed down the steep pathway until we reached the dirt track descending Durdle Fell.

He navigated the complex road with one hand on the wheel while he fiddled with the radio, but I wasn’t worried. He knew the mountain like the back of his hand and it wasn’t like he was stupid enough to white-knuckle it in a blizzard.

No, that would be me.

“What are you grinning about?” Fen treated me to a gentle smile of his own. “Not that I’m complaining. It looks good on you.”

“I was laughing at my own idiocy, as it goes. Can’t believe I thought it was a good idea to drag my heap of shit Fiesta up this road in the dark. I must’ve mistaken myself as a rally driver somewhere between here and the M6.”

“Yeah, I thought you’d lost the plot when I realised what you’d done.”

“You might’ve been right.”

“Have you found it yet?”

"The plot? Uh, that would be a hard nope. And it's hard to think up here when it's so far removed from my actual reality."

Fen sucked his teeth, finally settling on a crackly soft rock radio station. "Maybe you could flip that and take advantage of the change in perspective."

"Is that Officer Hawthorne talking?"

"They called me Mr Hawthorne inside, but yeah. And no. I'm not that person anymore, but I still think being up here could help you think if you let it."

"What makes you think I'm stopping it from helping me?"

"That's not what I said."

I gave him a look to let him know I'd caught the implication whether he'd meant to voice it or not.

Fen sighed. "Will you hate me if I'm brutally honest?"

"No. Bullshit annoys me."

"I told Dante Pope that the day before he met you for the first time. Do you know what he said?"

"What?"

"He said "that's why you like him, isn't it?" As if he could see into my damn mind."

I laughed. "Sounds like him."

"Still?"

"Yeah, but he's softer round the edges now. He's in love."

That earned me a quirked brow. Fen eased the Land Rover off the dirt track and onto an actual road. "Say what now?"

"He lives with the head gardener. They've been together since last summer."

The heart-warming gossip stunned Fen into silence, and a peaceful quiet fell over us as he drove into the village closest to Christmas Mountain. I discovered that I enjoyed his company as much when he didn't speak as when he did, and wasn't that just something? Most people annoyed me.

Fen didn't.

He excited me. Thrilled me, though it probably said more about me than him that I got giddy over him opening a tin of baked beans and banging them into a saucepan.

Right. It's the baked beans that make your heart thump like this.

Actually, it was. Because it was *everything* about Fen that lit me on fire, even the way he was chewing on his lip as we crossed the village boundary. *Leave that lip alone. It's mine.*

I laughed out loud this time.

Fen shot me a droll look. "You're the hottest weirdo I've ever met."

"I'm taking that to mean you don't meet a lot of hot people, because I know you've met a lot of weirdos."

"I don't meet many people at all around here. The closest I get are the haulage blokes who come to pick up the shipping loads."

"They're not hot?"

"Put it this way, the Christmas tree shipment we sent out this morning was picked up by a dude I thought might actually be Santa Claus."

"Ho ho ho."

"Very funny."

"I know. I missed a trick being a PO. I should've been on the telly."

"You have a great face for radio." Fen turned onto the main street of the quiet village.

It was busier than I expected, vehicles parked along both sides with near gridlock as cars tried to force their way down the middle in both directions. "Jesus. What's going on here?"

"You'll see."

"Sounds mysterious."

"Not really." Fen found a tiny spot and parallel parked his huge car with ease. It was so damn sexy I couldn't take my eyes off him.

"Is there anything you can't do?"

"Hmm?"

"Never mind." I wasn't about to tell him that a practical man who could do *anything* with his hands was my fucking jam. Maybe later, if the date played out.

But then...no. What were we going to do? Have a couple of drinks, then trip back to his place for a wild night in? As goddamn magical as that sounded, it couldn't happen. Something told me one taste of Fen Hawthorne would never be enough, and I had no plans on sticking around long enough for a second date. This one was symbolic—nostalgic, almost. Nothing else.

We exited the car onto the chaotic high street. Fen pointed north and gestured for me to follow him, which I did, all the while trying—and mostly failing—not to ogle the way his faded jeans hugged his thick legs. Taking in our surroundings was a healthy distraction—the bustle, the festive lights, and the scent of spicy baked goods in the air. "Why can I smell doughnuts?"

"Because they're everywhere," Fen said cryptically.

Or not that cryptically, as it turned out. The top of the street was a dead end by the primary school and the church. It was blocked off and set up as a Christmas market. A dinky doughnut stall was doing a roaring trade and every soul who passed me was carrying a paper cone of golf ball-sized treats dusted in cinnamon sugar. They really were everywhere.

"They smell like you," Fen whispered.

I spun to face him, but he'd picked up his pace, striding to the end of the market where most of the crowds were gathered. When I caught up to him, I saw why. Christmas trees, hundreds of them, filled the street, set out in a maze that laughing kids were buzzing around.

"It's our pop-up shop," he explained. "Saves local folk paying shipping fees if they don't want to schlep up the mountain, and brings people in from other places too."

"Doing your bit for the local economy?"

"Something like that, though it's more I don't have the time to dig idiots in cars they don't know how to drive out of the mud every ten minutes."

I'd never noticed before how soft-spoken Fen was. Despite his deep, masculine voice, he rarely swore or spoke with fire, unlike me who wouldn't have been out of place in a football firm. I liked it, his gentleness. It did something to me I couldn't explain. "I'd have called them worse than idiots."

He winked. "I know."

The Christmas tree shop was being run by the wives of the men who worked on the farm but lived in the town. "It's a good gig for them," Fen told me. "I pay them well so I don't have to worry about it if the weather keeps me on the fell."

"Does it do well? The tree business, I mean."

"Better than that. It makes more money in a month than everything else does all year round. Just as well, considering how much of my time the damn things take up."

"I've never thought about the day in the life of a Christmas tree farmer."

"Are you thinking about it now?"

More than you know. "A bit."

"Happy to show you. Just say the word."

The current between us flared to life again, but Fen was

called away before I could do something really stupid, like volunteer as tribute to be his constant companion.

He spent the next half hour loading huge trees onto the back of a lorry. I tried not to stare and wandered off to buy doughnuts and hot cider. Christmas wasn't usually my bag, but even my grumpy self found joy in spiced booze and cinnamon sugar. The brass band playing Christmas carols and the heavy scent of pine coating the air this close to the festive trees.

I need to buy Christmas presents. But I made no move to peruse the stalls filling the market.

I drank my cider and watched Fen instead, but somehow he still managed to surprise me when he joined me on the bench sometime later. "Did you save me a doughnut?"

"I did." I held out the bag. "You've got the good ones at the bottom with all the sugar."

"I'm sweet enough."

I was inclined to agree, but I kept that to myself as I watched Fen devour the doughnuts and lick sugar from his lips while I tracked his tongue.

He caught me watching. "See something you like?"

"What do you think?"

"I think this date is rubbish so far as all I've done is take you to work with me."

"Take me somewhere else then." *Take me to bed.* Wow. My imagination was on fire today.

Luckily, Fen didn't have X-ray vision into my brain. He held out his arm. I took it and let him tug me to my feet, and I didn't let go.

Neither did he. We walked arm-in-arm to the pub at the end of the road. It was as ready for Christmas as the rest of the village, though the music was fucking awful.

"Not a Wham! fan then?"

"Not unless you buy me another seven of those." I jerked my head at the pint of dark beer he'd set down in front of me. "I generally hate anything nice."

"Even me?"

"Except you."

"Good to know." Fen took a deep sip of his own beer, eyes dancing with mischief that looked much better on him than the conflict in his gaze when we'd talked about Dante Pope. It made me want to forget we'd known each other in a lifetime other than this, but because I was a wanker who could never let anything go, I picked at the festering wound. "Do you miss it?"

"Miss what?"

"Working in the prison. I know it ended, uh, badly, but you were so passionate about it."

"Was I?"

"Yeah. I mean, I always thought so. It was what made me like you so much. At the start, at least."

"What about after?"

"You were funny. And happy. It didn't seem to matter what hellish crap was going down in that place, you always managed to make me smile."

Fen traced a bead of condensation as it ran down his glass. "And what about now?"

"What do you mean?"

"What do you like about me now?"

"All of those things. Plus, you look amazing with a beard."

"So, all of those things exist without the uniform, right?"

"Right, but—"

"But nothing. What we do isn't who we are." Fen stood

abruptly and left the table we'd commandeered in a quiet corner.

He strode away, but I trusted him not to abandon me in Christmas Hell and gave him the space to do whatever he needed to do. It was a trick I'd learned from him, actually, the first time of many Dante Pope had shied away from me and walked out of our meetings. *"Give him space. He's a thinker. He'll come back once he figures out you're the best thing he could have on his side right now."*

It had taken Dante Pope two months to come back to me. I had faith Fen wouldn't make me wait that long.

He didn't.

A few minutes later, he returned with another bag of doughnuts. "Sorry."

"What for?"

"Flouncing off."

"No need. I knew it was dodgy ground when I brought it up."

"So? You shouldn't be afraid to have a simple conversation with me."

"I'm not afraid. You are."

Fen sighed. "I know."

He didn't elaborate, and I didn't make him. This was date night, not therapy.

We talked a little more about everything and nothing. I learned that he spent most summers rescuing his young trees from hungry rabbits. He asked me what I liked doing when I wasn't working or playing mums and dads.

It took me a while to remember. "Climbing, mainly. I used to train at the ju-jitsu gym, but I can't be arsed with the injuries these days. It's not a good look to rock up to an offender meeting with a shiner."

"I knew you were a fighter." Fen eyed me thoughtfully. "You had that don't-fuck-with-me vibe when you walked onto the wings, and no one ever did."

I enjoyed the way his deep voice wrapped around the word *fuck* way too much. Snorting out a laugh, I shook my head. "No one fucked with me because I always had a six-foot-four prison officer at my side."

"It wasn't always me."

"No, but was often enough that offenders knew we were friends."

"I didn't realise we were friends until I missed you so much." The admission seemed to take Fen by surprise. He glanced down at his hands, then curved them around his beer glass. "I should've given you my number that day, not trusted the assumption I'd see you again."

"You had no reason not to trust it. It wasn't like either of us knew Damon was going to die—not literally, anyway."

"Is that what happened?"

"It's why I didn't make it back to the prison when I said I would. I'm guessing you got hurt sometime after, because you were gone when I did come back and no one would talk about it."

"They're not allowed to," Fen said quietly. "There's still an investigation going on."

"Because someone fucked up?"

He shrugged. "I don't know. It's nothing to do with me—I, uh, don't remember most of it."

I took a breath. And a chance. I curled my leg around his beneath the table. "You want to talk about it?"

For a split second, I thought he might, then he shook his head, his expression somehow clearing and shuttering at the same time. "Not now. Back then, if I'd had someone in my life that got me like you do, maybe...I don't know."

He took refuge in his beer and I let him. It was cute that he thought I understood him, but far from accurate. I knew Fen Hawthorne was sweet and kind. I knew he flirted with me because he meant it.

I knew I wanted so much more.

7

Fen

I'd always known that dating Rami Stone—if that was even what this was—would be dangerous. I'd planned on buying him a couple of drinks, maybe a steak dinner, then driving him all the way back to the top of Christmas Mountain like a perfect gent, and yet here I was, three pints deep, my car long ago abandoned in the pub car park. "Why won't you let me buy you dinner?"

"Because you've cooked for me a thousand times—"

"Twice."

"—whatever. It's my turn to provide." Rami's smile was as sweet as he ever got, but it was genuine, and reminded me of the earnest probation officer I'd first met so long ago. The man who'd spend a whole day with an offender if they needed him to. Visit their grandmothers. Their aunties. Their long lost brothers and sisters who wanted nothing to do with them. It was why I'd wanted him for Dante Pope. Rami probably didn't know it, but I'd fought for him to be assigned that case, and not just because I wanted to spend time with him.

"Hey." Rami nudged me with his knee under the table. "If it's that important for you to be chivalrous, you can buy me a bag of chips."

"Hmm?"

He tilted his head. "You were miles away. Anywhere nice?"

Tempting as it was, I wasn't about to admit I'd been thinking about him. AKA wasting our time together when he was right here, in front of me, playing out the daydreams I'd carried all this time. "Probably not. And I'm not buying you chips for dinner. It's Christmas. You deserve better than that."

"It's not Christmas yet."

"It is in my world. Starts the day after Halloween and keeps going until midnight on Christmas Eve."

"You're still selling trees then?"

I nodded. "Last year, some drunk guy staggered to my front door and begged for a spare. Lucky for him, I had one and was sober enough to drive him home with it so he didn't get told off by his missus."

"He is lucky. That he found you, I mean. So am I."

"That a drunk bloke woke me up last Christmas?"

Rami rolled his eyes. "Don't be coy. It doesn't suit you."

"What does?"

"I couldn't say in such a public place." Rami winked and I felt heat rising in my bones.

Dangerous heat.

Delicious heat. I wasn't a man who thought with his dick, but something about *this* man made me see everything differently. I wanted every part of him I could have, even if it meant missing him harder when he was gone. "We never decided about dinner."

"*You* never decided. I'm happy with the chips."

I sighed. "Fine. Whatever. Chippie closes in ten minutes, so drink up."

Rami necked his beer, oblivious to my fascination with how his throat worked as he swallowed. It was elegant and filthy and did nothing to calm the smouldering in my belly.

I drank my beer too, enjoying the buzz as it joined the heat Rami's company had ignited. Then I dropped my empty glass onto the table. "Come on then."

"That a challenge?"

I stood. "Not one I'd win."

Rami chuckled and preceded me out of the pub, but I wasn't joking. Not really. I didn't have the first clue about his romantic history, but I was willing to bet he was better—or at least more well-versed—in any of this than I was, particularly the part that kept making his eyes darken and my heart beat faster. The *wanting* part. One-night stands weren't my thing, and he was leaving soon, so whatever fantasy was brewing in my overactive imagination couldn't happen.

But *Christ*, I wanted it to. So much. Almost enough for a seismic shift to occur in my soul so I could blink and be someone else. Someone who could take a man to bed and never see him again. Who could separate sexual attraction from the deeper longing I had for Rami.

The seismic shift didn't happen, though. And I didn't want it to. I was who I was. If chips and beer got out of hand, Rami would understand that. It was why I liked him so much; his ability to see beyond what people were to *who* they were.

You like his body too: his arms, his legs, his—

Wow. I'd never been so physically obsessed with

someone. It threw me for a loop, and by the time we reached the chip shop, I'd forgotten why we were there.

Rami shot me a look I couldn't fathom and ducked inside, leaving me to wander to the off-licence and buy more beer. In a daze, I grabbed a pack of cans from the shelf and paid for them, only realising when I was outside that I'd bought the super-strong stout my dad used to drink on Boxing Day to soften his hangover from the whisky-fuelled night before.

Oops. I traipsed back to the chip shop. Despite arguing against the chips, I couldn't deny the sight of Rami waiting outside, juggling big bags of chips skewered with giant battered sausages, was the stuff dreams were made of.

I approached him with what was probably the grin of a village idiot.

He smiled back. *Really* smiled, and I forgot for a moment that his presence in my life was temporary. That we didn't do lazy date nights like this all the time. *I want to kiss him.* The irony that he was standing beneath the chip shop's plastic mistletoe wreath just about killed me.

Yearning for his lips finished me off.

Rami's smile faded. "You okay?"

I held up the beer as my answer.

He cocked a dark brow. "They didn't have what you want?"

"What makes you say that?"

"You look disappointed."

"What, like, permanently? Thought you said I was Mr Happy?"

"At least I didn't call you Mr Hilarious, because I'd have been fucking lying."

"Oh yeah?"

"Yeah."

His deadpan humour flicked a switch in me, the switch controlling my base instincts. As the crackly radio in the chip shop banged out some Bing Crosby, I leaned in and kissed him, a soft brush of lips that didn't seem to surprise him.

Rami kissed me back, light and sweet. It wasn't the kind of kiss that matched the flirty banter we'd shared since forever ago, but it fit the mood and made me shiver. And, goddamn if I didn't want to do it a hundred times over.

The scent of chips brought me back to earth, reminding me that we weren't in a Christmas-themed fantasy land. We were kissing on the street of a rural northern village and even a hetero couple would've got some serious side-eye.

Chuckling, I pulled back. "Dinner looks good."

"Sure does." Rami tipped me a wink. "Where do you want to eat it?"

The playful suggestion dancing in his voice was another reminder that the simplistic beauty of a stolen kiss was a big fat lie. There was nothing simple about kissing Rami. It made me want to do things I couldn't do if he was serious about walking out of my life again, and I couldn't reconcile the two parts of myself. They didn't fit. Or maybe they did, and that was the problem—that I didn't know myself as well as I thought I did.

You know you want him. That should be enough. And it was. I just couldn't...have him.

Not for one night.

Rami nudged me, bringing me back to the present. He'd asked me a question and I'd failed to answer.

I considered our options. It was arctic-cold out, but the sky was clear and I didn't mind a bit of chill. In truth, in Rami's company, with the kiss we'd shared still tingling on my lips, I barely felt it, and I couldn't help but wonder if his undone coat and bright eyes were a sign he felt the same. "We could walk and eat? If you don't mind chow on the move."

"Works for me." He passed me a bag of chips. "I went heavy on the vinegar. That okay?"

"Marry me," I said absently, still thinking about kissing him until it dawned on me what I'd said. "I mean, for the chip-doctoring alone."

Rami snorted.

I threw a chip at him. "You don't think that's important?"

He evaded my spud missile and stuffed one of his own into his mouth. "It's important," he said around chewing. "But I can think of better reasons for marrying you."

In the split second it took me to digest that, he crossed the road, leaving me to trail after him, the beer bag swinging from my wrist. By the time I caught up with him, the moment had passed.

We walked in a companionable quiet, not quite silent, but without meaningless small talk too. I'd always known Rami as a man who didn't speak without reason and that apparently hadn't changed. He said things that mattered, and listened when others spoke. It was what made him so good at his job, and it was strange to see how his patience back then didn't entirely translate into his personal life now. Or maybe I was witnessing the damage the past few years had inflicted on him. *He lost his brother and gained responsibility for a baby. I'm surprised he's not wrinkled and grey.*

Not that I'd have cared if he was. The Rami Stone aesthetic was about far more than how he looked.

"You're a dreamer."

A chip hit the side of my face.

I blinked.

Rami laughed. "See?"

"I see you laughing."

"Oh yeah?"

"Yeah. You're pretty."

Rami rolled his eyes, balled his chip paper up, and stuffed it into his coat pocket. "My first comment stands."

Of course it did, and he wasn't wrong. Every school report I'd ever brought home had said the same thing. I shrugged. "Dreaming is good for the soul."

"So is beer."

Rami raided the bag on my wrist and retrieved a can of extra-strong beer. He read the label and his brows rose in a dark wave. "Trying to get me drunk?"

"Not on purpose. You might have to stay over if we finish those, though. I'll be too drunk to walk you home."

"I can walk myself home."

"In the dark? Up a mountain you don't know? Yeah...I'm not letting you do that."

"Letting me?" Rami laughed again from deep in his belly, oblivious to the sweet shiver it sent down my spine. "Though I suppose you could stop me doing just about anything if you put your brawn to good use."

"You don't think hefting trees around is good use?"

"It's not the *only* good use. That's my point." Rami's gaze glittered with heat and I felt conflict rage inside me again, but I ignored it this time. Curbing the flirting when I'd already put my lips on him tonight seemed kind of pointless.

And I didn't want to, so there was that.

I finished my chips and opened a beer, pointing it at him as if the sight of it would convince him that hiking up the mountain by himself was absolutely not happening. "Okay, let's take the word 'letting' out of the equation, but you still can't walk home in the dark, with or without me once I drink this, so it's up to you…"

"In what sense?"

"Should I drink it or not?"

Rami stopped walking and caught my elbow, forcing me to do the same. "Are you asking me to stay the night?"

Am I? The literal answer was yes, but that wasn't what he was asking me. "I am asking you to stay the night," I said slowly, popping the top on my beer, though I didn't drink any…*yet.* "And I don't want you to sleep in the spare room."

Rami tilted his head sideways. "Why do I sense a big fat *but* in that sentence?"

He didn't seem overly concerned. Maybe I was angsting about nothing. Either way, I was about to find out. "There's no *but*…exactly, I, uh, I'm not into one-night stands, so…"

A slow grin warmed Rami's face. "So, you're asking me to sleep with you but not sleep with you?"

"Something like that. I mean, I'm not saying *nothing* would happen, I'm just not into fucking around—I don't enjoy it."

"That's the first time I've ever heard you say fuck."

"That's what you're taking from what I said?"

Rami tipped beer down his throat, watching me as he swallowed, molten gaze sinking into me. "Mostly. The rest isn't something you have to worry about. I'd be totally into fucking around if you were too, but I don't need it. Shit, I haven't shared a bed with an adult for more than a year and it's not the sex I miss."

"What is it then?"

He drank more beer and nudged my can to my lips, sealing our fate to spend the entire night together. "It's the warmth," he said, quiet and low. "That feeling when you know someone's behind you, or you have your arms around them from behind—that skin-on-skin, *man*, I love that."

"Me too. But just so you know, if you were sticking around longer than a couple of days? Yeah, I'd totally bang you."

A silence fell over us that was so intense I could hardly breathe. Rami stared me down, and I sank into his addictive gaze like I was walking on quicksand. Something drew us together, one step, and then two, until we were nose to nose, and we should've been kissing, but we weren't.

Yet.

Rami took a breath. "You make it hard to remember I have an entire life to get back to in Manchester. I feel like a different man up here."

"A better man?"

"Who's to say? All I know is I want to spend this night with you and not think about what comes next."

There was good and bad in that statement, but I was tipsy enough to latch onto what I wanted to hear and ignore what I didn't. I drank more beer, then I found his hand and tugged him in the direction of our long trek home. "Less thinking more walking then."

He laughed. "Right."

8

Rami

Hand in mine, Fen led me all the way to his rustic house on the mountain. In the dark and half pissed, it was a tough hike, but Fen's presence distracted me from the fact that my exercise regime was half what it had been before Charlie had come along. He didn't say much, but he didn't have to, his quiet good humour was enough.

We reached his house in the dead of night—at least, it felt that way. In truth, I had no idea what the time was, and I didn't much care. It didn't seem important. I fired off a text to let Safia know I wasn't coming home, then dropped my phone into my pocket and instantly forgot about it.

We'd drunk all our beer on the way home. It was *strong*, but the cold night air had kept me sober enough to still have my faculties. I wasn't sure about Fen. He was hard to read. Perhaps that was why I'd never matched his flirtatious behaviour with a man who didn't dig one night stands. *Is he demi-sexual?* No. Maybe. I didn't know. But that didn't seem to

106

matter much either. Whatever was brewing between us, we'd figure it out.

Or we wouldn't, and I'd go home, and my life would carry on without him.

Ugh. That wasn't a pleasant thought, but lucky for me, I was an expert at sticking my head in the sand, so I did just that and focused on the reality that was Fen unlocking his front door and ushering me inside.

I shut the door behind us and watched Fen kick off his boots and pad to the kitchen. His earlier words echoed in my head: "*...just so you know, if you were sticking around longer than a couple of days? Yeah, I'd totally bang you.*" With that knowledge rattling in my brain, watching him move around his tiny kitchen like a graceful bear was harder—no pun intended—than I'd anticipated. He was so fucking sexy, but more than that, he was...lovely. I'd never understood that word before, but as I observed him from my post at the front door, its definition solidified.

Fen opened a cupboard and retrieved a whisky bottle. He set it on the table, then glanced up and caught my gaze on him. "Nightcap?"

His smirk hit differently now I knew where his head was at, connecting to a deeper part of me I'd forgotten existed. I took my shoes off and shrugged out of my coat, hanging it beside Fen's. Then I drifted to his side like I was walking on air and claimed my whisky glass. "You're not making it easy for me to contain myself."

"Whisky makes you horny?"

"You do," I clarified. "The whisky just makes it harder for me to swallow it down."

Fen sighed. "I don't want you to feel oppressed."

"I don't. No one ever died from delaying instant gratification."

"Good to know."

I sipped my whisky, letting the burn seep into me as Fen flicked the lights on his glorious Christmas tree. "Is it?"

"Yeah. Maybe. Actually, I don't know. I've never thought about it as much as I have since you showed up. Before that, it wasn't so tangible that I had to talk about it. I just knew I didn't enjoy sex with men I wasn't emotionally attached to and I can't have casual sex with my friends."

There were two ways I could've taken that. One that he wasn't emotionally attached enough to me to have sex with me, the other that we were so friendly now that he never would. Neither option sat well with me, but I could live with the second. Being friends with Fen forever far outweighed fucking him once and losing him.

It also occurred to me that we were overthinking something that hadn't happened. I was leaving soon, and he'd offered me the privilege of his company on what would have otherwise been a long and lonely night. *Enjoy him. This might not ever happen again.*

I drank my whisky.

Fen drank his too, then he took my hand and led me upstairs. Despite knowing we weren't going to fuck, it was still a goddamn thrill. And his bedroom had a zen vibe that settled the scratchy feeling I'd carried for months and months and months before I'd landed on Christmas Mountain. I leaned in the doorway, watching him unbutton his flannel shirt and unbuckle his belt. "How naked are we getting for this?"

"How naked do you want to be?" Fen shot me a look over

his shoulder. "But you should know, the only pyjamas I own are the ones your sister tried to knit me last year."

I winced. "That doesn't sound good."

"She's a better cook, put it that way."

I didn't want to think about my sister right now. I waved away the notion of pyjamas and ventured farther into the room. Fen was by the window. I joined him and finished unbuttoning his shirt, revealing a plain T-shirt underneath.

Both had to go. If we weren't going to fuck, I at least needed to feel his warm skin against mine.

I stripped Fen to his underwear and resisted, just, the urge to stare at the bulge within his black boxer-briefs. "How naked do you want *me*?"

Fen undressed me, keeping his gaze locked with mine, drinking in my shiver as his fingertips grazed my skin. He took me down to my underwear, levelling the playing field without a glance south. I wondered for a minute if he simply didn't feel what I felt, then he closed his eyes, sucking in a deep breath. "Don't ever think I don't want you."

"I don't think that." I stepped closer and put my hands on his shoulders. The movement brought us chest to chest, and the moment his skin touched mine something within me shifted and I knew I'd never be the same again. Goddamn. My heart had never beat so fast. So loud. And I'd never wanted something I couldn't have so fucking much.

Fen opened his eyes. His cobalt gaze took me prisoner. Held me hostage. He smiled, the fucker, as if he sensed the volcanic inferno I was trying to suppress. "Can I kiss you again?"

"You don't need to ask."

"No?"

"No." I took matters into my own hands and sealed my mouth to his, claiming his lips.

I had sweet intentions, but my tongue had other ideas. It slipped into his mouth of its own accord, and he didn't fight me. He brought his strong arms around me like a cage and kissed me back, cupping the nape of my neck with one big hand while the other gripped my hip.

I groaned against his lips. Christ, was he trying to kill me? If he was, it wasn't a bad way to go. Kissing him was everything, and the sensation of his broad torso crushed against me was the icing on a cake I'd eat every day if I could.

Fen backed us up until we reached his bed. We tumbled down, but before I could land on him and amp things up to a level I lacked the strength to resist, I angled my fall to lie next to him.

It worked, kind of, if I counted grinding my hard cock into his leg any kind of restraint.

We kissed for hours. Fen explored every inch of my skin with his big, calloused hands, and I let my lips travel down his throat and to his chest, all the while fighting to keep my dick to myself.

It didn't help that the bulge in his underwear was probably visible from space. I ached to touch it, to trail a finger from root to tip, to grip it, to squeeze and taste it. Like, literally ached. Could a man get cramp in his cock? It sure fucking felt like it.

Either way, I didn't touch his dick. I kissed him for as long as we could stay awake, then I fell asleep with him wrapped around me from behind like the dream fantasy I'd described to him on the way home. It wasn't the all night fuck I'd imagined when my attraction to him had manifested so long ago, but if it was the end of our story, I could take it.

Perfection was hard to discount.

🎄

Woodstock by Joni Mitchell woke me. At first, I thought I was still dreaming, helped along by the sensation of Fen's big body behind me, but as the gentle melody and lyrics seeped into me, his bedroom solidified and I realised it was the alarm on his phone.

Cute. I shut it off, half convinced I'd sleepwalked into a Tardis and woken in the wrong decade, and I wasn't sad about it. My mum had told me once I'd been born with an old soul, and I could dig it.

Fen's chest pressed to my back?

Yeah. I could dig *that* sometime until forever, and so I didn't move, not for a long while until it occurred to me that his alarm had been set for a reason.

Sighing, I forced myself to roll over. Fen let me go, his arms loose and clumsy. He was dead asleep, and fuck me if he wasn't the most beautiful sight. His ashy hair was a riot, his face relaxed and boyish, and though I missed his sparkly gaze, without it, I almost forgot that Fen Hawthorne was such a complex creature.

Huh. Maybe I was about the simple life after all.

Whatever. Waking him felt like a sin. The bad kind. Not the kind that was still making my balls ache. The only upside was I'd get to see him smile. Maybe. If he was pleased to wake up and find me in his bed, and not perplexed by a beer-fuelled mistake.

It wasn't a mistake. My gut and my heart knew it, but I was nervous all the same.

I raised a shaky hand and cupped his jaw, revelling in the

feel of his velvety beard against my palm. It was just the right length—like thick, lush scruff. I let my thumb stroke one cheekbone and softly kissed the other. "Fen?"

Nothing. Not even a flicker. I tried again, a slow grin building on my face, splitting it in half.

Still nothing.

I moved to shake him, but a new sound from his phone made me jump out of my skin, a different song, this time— Sleigh Ride by Ella Fitzgerald at seventeen times the volume of Joni Mitchell. "Jesus fucking Christ!"

Fen's eyes flew open. He seized my wrists and bolted upright, taking me with him. "What? What is it?"

"Your alarm," I said dryly. "It's louder than Satan's Saturday night lock-in."

"Oh." Fen blinked hard, clearing sleep from his brain. "Damn. Sorry. Where's my phone?"

"Here." I wrestled a hand free and passed it to him, half amused at his rude awakening, and half endeared by his reaction to it. "Sorry if I made you jump. It scared the hell out of me."

Fen swiped at the screen. "I thought I turned it off."

"Which one?"

"What?"

"It went off a while ago too—Joni Mitchell. I liked that one better."

Fen laughed, low and deep. "That's my reward if I get up on the first go. If I don't, I get blasted with whatever tune Addie decides I should suffer. It's his favourite game with me."

"It's a good game." I was so enamoured by Fen's relationship with my sister's kids I found it hard to breathe when they talked about him and he wasn't there. But safe in bed with him, I could appreciate it for what it was: fucking beautiful. "He threw pig shit at my head, so I think you got the better deal."

"Oh, he does that to me too."

"Damn. I thought I was special."

"You are."

Just like that, the intensity of the night before returned, blanketing us in heat and want and the fate that had brought us together again. I was still so hot for him, but in the growing light of the early morning, it was more than that. Fen was my friend, and waking up with him like this was so perfect I wouldn't have changed a thing.

I gave him a hug he wasn't expecting, latching our bodies together in all the right places. I was hard. So was he. But doing nothing about it felt right.

He wove his hand into the hair at the nape of my neck, massaging the base of my skull. I sighed with a contentment I hadn't felt in years, if ever, and I found myself glad I wasn't waking up to do the walk of shame up Christmas Mountain because this was so much better.

I pressed my face into the warmth of where his shoulder joined his neck. "Do you have to be somewhere this morning?"

"Soon," he said with regret. "I mean, I'm the boss so I can do what I like, but we're crazy busy right now. I need to be there."

I hummed my acceptance, knowing that in actual fact, I needed to be somewhere else too. Charlie had slipped into Safia's chaotic family as though he'd always been there, but he still looked for me every few minutes, seeking reassurance that I wasn't going to disappear like everyone else in his life had done.

The thought of not being there when he woke drove me out of Fen's arms and upright again.

He rubbed my back. "Something bothering you?"

"Charlie. He doesn't know I won't be there."

Fen nodded. "Get in the shower. I'll get the breakfast on then I'll drive you home."

"You don't have to do that."

"So? I'm doing it anyway."

I had no argument. I took a quick—and cold—shower, then let him feed me a bacon sandwich before he drove me up the mountain in one of the farm's vehicles.

He stopped in the turning circle by the gate. There was no one around, save a few goats shouting at the birds, and I was glad of it. I wanted him all to myself just a little while longer.

I turned to face him, drinking him in. While I'd showered, he'd put himself back together. His hair was no longer wild and his bright eyes were clear. "God, you're so fucking hot."

It wasn't what I meant to say, and I needed him to know I craved so much more about him than that, but such was my life up here in this goddamn mountain, it fell out of me before I could catch it.

Fen grinned, full lips turning up enough to make his whole face light up. "You're not bad yourself."

"Thanks."

"No. Thank *you*. I had the perfect night. I never got round to asking you if you wanted more because I was so fixated on telling you I didn't, but having you in my bed was everything. I hope you know that."

"I do."

There was so much more I could've said, but words didn't seem enough.

Fen didn't seem to have many either. He kissed my cheek

and then my lips, and then his phone rang, reality, perhaps, calling us home.

I kissed him back and got out of the car with no promises of when I'd see him again. My heart was conflicted as I walked away. I already missed him, but those precious hours I'd spent with him would stay with me forever.

▲

Charlie was waiting for me in the hallway, half dressed in outdoor clothes, one wellie boot on his foot. Mae was a little ahead of him, charging for the front door.

I caught her, swinging her up to one hip and collecting Charlie to sit on the other. "Where's the fire?"

Charlie slow blinked as if he'd just woken up—he'd inherited my dislike of early mornings.

Mae poked me in the ribs with the magic wand she was carrying. "Uncle Fen's here. Let me down."

Oh. "He's not here anymore, bug. He just left."

Mae's face fell. "Why?"

"He had to work."

Mae stuck her bottom lip out. With any other child I'd have been worried they were about to unleash a serious dose of the waterworks, but Mae McCade was my sister's child and I was fairly sure her main emotions were mischief and rage.

She wriggled free of my hold and darted to the front door, hurling it open hard enough to smash against the wall. The rumble of Fen's car engine could still be heard, but he was nowhere in sight and this kid legit *growled*, turning on me with a face of thunder. "He's gone!"

I didn't point out that I'd already told her that. If she'd really been my sister, she'd have kicked me in the balls.

Instead, I pointed at the kitchen. "Do you want chocolate on toast for breakfast?"

Just call me Super Nanny. Mae forgot Fen and ran like a hurricane to the kitchen. I followed with Charlie and dug Safia's secret stash of Nutella out of the top cupboard.

She made bread every day. I cut child-sized slices from yesterday's loaf and threw them on the Aga wondering, for the thousandth time, how my life had morphed into a scene from a Hallmark film.

"I don't want bananas." Mae thwacked the back of my legs with her wand. "They're yucky."

"I didn't say anything about bananas."

"Mummo makes us eat them."

"I'm not your mum."

"You're too hairy," Addie supplied from behind me. He wandered into the kitchen, rubbing his eyes. "But she said to tell you you're looking after us this morning while she has a bath and shaves her legs."

"Nice. Where's your baby sister?"

"With Mummo. She's asleep."

Addie slid into a chair at the table. I made extra toast for him, slathered the lot in sugary chocolatey crap without a single piece of fruit in sight. Yep. Definitely Super Nanny.

We made it through breakfast without any tears, not even mine. Addie cleaned up while I dressed Charlie and failed in every attempt to convince Mae that her wizard costume wasn't the best outfit for feeding the pigs.

"They like Mrs Wizard. I cast spells to make them fatter."

Okay. Whatever. She won. I lost. But I couldn't deny that a morning in the company of three small humans who didn't give a tiny fuck about things that were supposedly important was refreshing. We fed pigs, painted pictures, and rinsed our way through the household DVD collection. Maybe I should've taken them outside more, but they had Paddy for that. I was the fun uncle who let them eat shit and nap on the couch.

I was halfway to a snooze myself when Safia and Paddy came downstairs from what was clearly a morning well spent.

Safia took over the childcare. I made my escape and Paddy walked with me back to the log cabin.

"It's nice having another adult around." He cast me a sideways glance I chose to ignore on principle that he'd just had the time of his life banging my sister. "Gives Safia a break."

"From you?"

"Very funny. No, I mean from running around after Addie and Mae. In case you haven't noticed, they're, uh, lively."

"They're fucking feral."

Paddy grinned, proud.

I couldn't help but grin back, even if his attempts at being subtle were northside of pathetic. "They're great kids. Charlie laughs a lot around them."

"So do you."

"Do I?"

"No offence, bro, but I figured you'd be in a foul mood the entire time you were here, and you haven't been."

"Maybe you're a crap judge of character then."

"Or maybe you like it here." Paddy spread his hands as we reached the log cabin. "Just putting it out there."

"Why?"

"Why do you think?"

"Because you have a misguided notion that I can uproot my life and bring my work to a place that can't stream the fucking news channel. Even if I could make it work remotely—"

"You told Safia last year you could."

"—what? No, I didn't."

"Yes, you did."

I loved my brother-in-law, but I wanted to punch him right now. "No, I didn't. I told her I could work from home half of the week, but the rest of it I'd have to get childcare for because I can't exactly visit a fucking prison with a toddler on my hip."

"Do something else then. You're a qualified counsellor. You could do that. Or teach."

"What if I don't want to? What if I'm perfectly happy with my life the way it is?"

Paddy snorted. "Lad, you haven't been happy since you wound up in Manchester babysitting Damon in the first place."

"Lad?"

"I'm northern. I don't mean nothing by it."

I knew he didn't, but he'd caught me off guard with his bargain basement life-coaching session and I was a grumpy bastard at the best of times. *Not when you're with Fen.* But that was easy to say when I'd spent a fraction of my life in his company. Give it six months. I was willing to bet he wouldn't like me so much by the end of it.

"Earth to Rama." Paddy waved his hand in front of my face.

I didn't punch him. Just. "What?"

"I'm just saying, if you genuinely don't want to be up here, that's fine, but if it's logistics stopping you, don't let it. We can work it out."

"You can't "work out" anything with your crappy Internet

up here and that shit is non-negotiable for me. I'm not a farmer, dude. If the last few days have taught you anything, it must be that."

I was done with the conversation. I softened the growl in my tone with a forced smile and shouldered the door to the log cabin.

It swung shut in Paddy's face and I wasn't sad about it. At least, not at first. By the time I realised I was a moody twat, he was long gone.

Sighing, I threw myself on the bed and shut my eyes. For months and months and months, I'd been so tired that snatched sleep at any opportunity had been the only thing keeping me going, but I'd slept like a baby in Fen's arms, and the slumber-fuelled reprieve I craved now wouldn't come. All I saw were the faces that surrounded me here—Safia, Paddy, Addie, and Mae. Baby Lalla. Charlie. Fen. I didn't know any of them as much as I wanted to, but that was just life, right?

It's the life you made. If you don't like it, change it.

Easier said than done. Even if I conceded Paddy's observation that kicking it in the wilderness was more fun that suffering the rat race in the city, my point about me lacking outdoor skills—and inclination—along with his fucking terrible Internet service still stood. My work was important to me. I didn't know who I was without it.

Despite feeling wide awake, I dozed off. I woke to Paddy standing over me, kicking my legs with his giant booted feet. "Get dressed. I've got something to show you."

I sat up, blinking. "I am dressed."

"I meant your feet. Put your boots on."

"Safia's boots, you mean."

"All right, lad. Just get on with it."

I did as I was told. Paddy was the good cop in his and

Safia's comedy double act, but he was a tenacious bastard when he had something on his mind.

Grumbling, I stamped into my borrowed boots and joined him at the door. He handed me a coat that wasn't mine. "We're going for a walk."

"Where to?"

"To the solution to all your problems."

"That's a bold statement."

Paddy grunted and set off towards the path that descended the mountain on the opposite side of Fen's house. It was a steep path, rocky and rough. Paddy had built a sturdy gate at the top that he kept bolted to keep his unruly kids and wandering pigs safe. Only the goats could come and go as they pleased.

He opened it and waved me through. I preceded him along the path until we came to a high stile. Fen's name was carved into the old wood, alongside *Cheryl* and *Daisy*.

"Cheryl's the sister, Daisy's the dog," Paddy said to my frown.

"I didn't know he had a sister," I replied absently, tracing the carving with my fingertip. I knew about the family dog, though. There were pictures in Fen's house.

"Thought you two were friends?" Paddy hopped over the stile. "Or whatever a naughty slumber party makes you."

I tossed him a scowl. "Shut your face. It wasn't like that."

Paddy smirked.

I glowered harder. "It wasn't. We got pissed in town and he said it was safer for me to stay over than wander up the mountain and die."

"Well, he wasn't wrong about that. Not sure I believe you about the rest of it."

"I don't give a shit what you believe."

I delivered my words with a smile for no other reason than snapping at Paddy was like kicking a Labrador—horrible. And I didn't have the headspace for more guilt, even though his answering grin let me know I hadn't hurt his feelings.

We traversed the mountain path into a headwind. It whipped around my ears, searing my exposed skin with cold the way it had done that fateful night I'd arrived. It was hard to believe how little time had passed since then. It felt like eons. "Are you going to tell me where we're going?"

Paddy pointed ahead. "Down there."

"Hilarious. Anywhere in particular, or are you hoping to lose me in the forest?"

"As if Fen wouldn't find you."

"Maybe he wouldn't want to."

"Yeah. Okay." Paddy's scepticism was likely visible from the moon, but he let it pass and kept pointing forward. "We're going to Isaac Hawthorne's treehouse."

He'd have surprised me less if he'd said we were visiting the queen at Balmoral. "What?"

"You heard me."

"That doesn't make it make sense."

"It doesn't have to make sense. Not until you see it."

Wonderful. My scowl returned tenfold, but there was little I could do but keep following Paddy down the mountain until we came to a levelled-out clearing. Surrounded by trees, I didn't realise how big it was at first, but as we continued forward, I saw the ledge in the mountain was pretty vast.

It was covered in dense pine trees—at least, I figured them for pine. My tree knowledge was fairly limited. Either way, it was green and lush and felt as much like Narnia as the rest of Christmas Mountain.

I couldn't see a treehouse, though.

"Look up," Paddy said helpfully.

I gave him the finger, then tilted my head to the sky. A construction that wouldn't have looked out of place in a fairy tale greeted me. Made of wood and glass, it was built into the biggest tree I'd ever seen in real life, high above us, accessible by a wide staircase made from knotted wood and rope. "The hell is this?"

"Told you," Paddy said. "It's Isaac Hawthorne's treehouse."

"It's...epic."

"Wait till you see inside." Grinning, Paddy led the way to the bottom of the staircase. "It's a bit wobbly, but you're not scared of heights, right?"

I wasn't, but there was something intimidating about climbing stairs that had once belonged to Fen's father. I couldn't say why. There just was. And, actually, the wind rocking the wood beneath my feet had the potential to be terrifying if I hadn't been so terminally curious about what lay ahead.

We reached the top. Paddy waved me forward to a rustic door and handed me a key. "I don't know why we keep it locked. It's not like we're going to get burgled."

"It belongs to you now?"

"To be honest, we're not sure. The land deeds are pretty vague and the key was in the house when we moved in."

"So it could be Fen's?"

Paddy shrugged. "Maybe. He's never mentioned it."

"You haven't thought to ask him?"

"I'm a busy man."

I snorted and unlocked the door. "You could've asked his dad when you bought the land."

"We didn't know it was here and he never mentioned it either."

"How do you know it was his then?"

"You'll see."

Paddy waved me forward. I turned my back on him and ventured into the treehouse. More wood greeted me, rustic and glorious, and I found myself in what was, in effect, a bedsit. There was a kitchenette, a tiny bathroom, and a leather futon, and then taking up most of the space was a desk built from a tree trunk with cast-iron legs.

The desk was by the window. From the solid wood chair, the view stretched for miles through the dense forest and beyond. It was beautiful, but I was still confused. "Why are you showing me this?"

"Because..." Paddy spun in a slow circle, then settled his gaze on a cupboard tucked against the high wooden ceiling of the treehouse. It was a stretch even for him to reach it, and I expected it to reveal something completely ridiculous—this was Paddy, after all, the man who'd sent me a wooden stag head the size of a small bungalow for my birthday—but inside was a satellite Internet router that looked as though it'd been built for NASA. "This here," Paddy said, smirking at the way my eyebrows were fast disappearing into my hair, "was Isaac's answer to building a global distribution network in the middle of nowhere."

"How do you know that?"

"Because he left a manifesto on how to do it." Paddy stretched, reached into the cupboard—just—and retrieved a leather-bound notebook. "I mean, I say manifesto, it's three pages of instructions of how to make the thing work, but he built the network Fen's still using today, so I figure it panned out."

I took the notebook from him and flipped through the pages. The handwriting was eerily familiar. I wondered where I'd seen it before, then remembered the offender files I'd trawled through that had been filled with Fen's similar scrawl and my heart skipped a beat. In a place where I was surrounded by his family history, somehow this hit hard.

The instructions were laced with the same brevity Fen had used in his offender reports—no wasted words or superfluous detail. Pure fact. Apparently it was a Hawthorne thing, and carrying that knowledge made me feel closer to Fen, despite the fact that I was going to leave him soon.

"So..." Paddy said.

I'd forgotten he was there. I blinked and turned to him. "What?"

"So what do you think?"

"About what?"

Paddy's face folded into an expression that was close to a glare as he ever got. "About the office. The Internet. And what you could use it for."

"Me?"

"Yes. You. All that stuff you said about not being able to stay here longer than a week because you needed the Internet to work remotely. You could do that here."

Oh. I'd been so wrapped up in thinking about Fen, I hadn't thought about the practicalities of the office in the sky and what it could mean for me. And aside from arguing with Safia about it, I'd tried not to think about work at all. My job was consuming when I allowed it to be, and recently I'd had too much grief in my personal life to let that happen. I loved my work, but perhaps the truth was I already had one foot out the door. "I guess I could use it to catch up with my inbox. It's taking two hours to update on my phone."

"Try it." Paddy stretched again and fiddled with the satellite router. A couple of green lights flashed. "There. It's on."

"Do you need a password to connect to it?"

"How would I know?"

"Thought you had the answers to all my problems?"

"You could always ask Fen."

Paddy gave me a sly look.

I gave him my middle finger and fished my phone from my pocket.

Paddy snorted and made for the door. "I've got goats to round up. Good luck with everything."

He disappeared before I could contemplate what *"everything"* meant. Gaze fixed on my phone, I wandered to the futon and sat. Even lagging behind in updates, my inbox was ridiculous. My saving grace was that the offenders I was currently supervising were coming to the end of their probation and no longer required as much attention. Most had one face-to-face meeting left with me, and a handful of calls I could do over Zoom if Isaac's wonder satellite worked as well as I needed it to.

The Zoom calls were unnecessary, but they made me feel better about the fact that I was miles away from being close enough to reach my offenders if they needed me, and that perhaps I had been for a while now.

It's not like you abandoned them. You kept your list small so you could focus on them and Charlie at the same time. You've never missed an appointment or not been there in a crisis.

But I wasn't there now. And if I gave what Safia, Paddy, and Fen were saying serious thought, the reality was I'd never be there for them again.

So? They won't need you forever.

But maybe I needed them. *Maybe*, my work as a probation officer was so rooted into my DNA by now that I couldn't give it up.

It's just a job.

Damn, Safia was loud, even when she was somewhere else.

I opened the connections menu on my phone and searched for the satellite router. My cynicism was so strong I expected it not to be there, but it appeared in seconds as *HAWTHORNE TREEHOUSE.* I swallowed hard and clicked on it. It connected and my phone was suddenly alive with activity. Notifications. Emails. Missed messages. I couldn't take it all in.

So I didn't. I opened my inbox and ignored everything else.

Two hours later, I was caught up and had requested a Zoom meeting with my supervisor.

She called thirty seconds later, her face filling my phone screen with a WhatsApp video call.

I answered with more than a little trepidation. "Hi, Monica."

She smiled and in my heart, a tiny seed sprouted green shoots.

9

Fen

There was something wrong with me. Okay. Maybe not wrong, but definitely different. Last week's me wouldn't have found himself fetching someone's repaired car from the better-equipped garage he'd taken it to without telling them and driving it home, but that was exactly what I did with Rami's beat-up Fiesta.

You're manipulating the situation so he has to see you.

Couldn't deny it. My tenuous excuse was that he'd given me the impression that he wanted to. And, he seemed to have forgotten about his car, though why I was making it easier for him to leave, I had no idea.

Because you're a genius, that's why.

Gold star.

I parked Rami's car outside my house—whatever my motives, I still had little faith that it would make it all the way up the mountain. Then I played a game of chicken with my phone, knowing I should text him but not knowing quite what to say.

Ultimately, I lost. And I wasn't good at doing nothing, so when my work for the day was done, I drove the damn Fiesta up Christmas Mountain like a good lumberjack to deliver the news in person.

Safia met me at the gate. She was clutching a plate of mince pies, the good ones laced with cherry brandy and wrapped in the almond pastry my dad had taught her to make a month before he'd died. It was a Hawthorne special and I was so happy this chaotic little family had come to our land to keep it alive.

My stomach was glad too. I ate two on the spot, then relieved her of the plate. "Did you see me coming or hear my belly grumbling?"

"Both." Safia winked. "And actually, I suspected it wouldn't be long before I saw you today."

"Why's that?"

"Because you kept my brother out all night."

She winked again. I pulled a face and ate another pie— my standard reaction to most things. Praise the Lord I didn't have a sedentary desk job. "I kept him safe, not out. Did you want him to climb the fell after a skinful?"

"I wanted him to have fun."

"And did he?"

"You tell me."

"No." I finished stuffing my face and handed Safia the plate. "I did bring his car back, though. It's fixed."

"Oh."

Safia's face looked like I felt: unenthused. *No one wants him to go. Why can't he just stay?* How I was so convinced I needed that after so little time with him, I couldn't say, but I. Did. Not. Want. Him. To. Leave.

But it wasn't my place to beg him to stay. It was Safia's, and I got the feeling she'd already tried and failed, and wasn't that a depressing thought? "Where is he, anyway? I have the bill for him."

"Ah, he already told you not to pay it for him, eh?"

I shrugged. Whatever conversations I'd had with Rami, I knew better than to force that situation on him. He was an adult, which equalled his car, his problem. I'd got him a deal, though, and the invoice stuffed in my pocket—*which you could just give to Safia, you fool*—was half what it would've been in Manchester.

"He's, uh, in the treehouse," Safia said.

My brows cinched in confusion. "My dad's old office?"

"Yeah. The key was in the house. I probably should've mentioned it a lifetime ago, but it's not on the deeds, so we weren't sure who it belonged to, and then it never came up, and too much time had passed without it being weird—"

I held up a hand to stop her. "It's not on the deeds because that land doesn't belong to anyone, not me, not you. My dad built his office there because it was the best place for the satellite signal, but he couldn't sell it to you because the tree it's housed in didn't technically belong to him. To be honest, I have a good enough router in the main house these days that I pretty much forgot about it."

"Oh." Safia blew out a breath. "Well, that's all right then. Here was me thinking we'd accidentally stolen it from you."

"Wouldn't care if you had. It's just a shed in the sky."

"Is it?" Safia gave me a shrewd stare.

I stared her down, not in the mood to play games. "It isn't NASA. My dad used it to play online chess with his mate in

Bermuda while the rest of us thought he was doing the accounts."

"Your pops was a clever man."

I couldn't argue with that. Or wait much longer to lay eyes on Rami. This morning seemed a long time ago.

Ignoring Safia's amusement, I left her at the gate and traipsed across her property to the trail on the other side of the mountain. It was a path I rarely trod. The forest was thick and lush on the northern side, but wild and free. We didn't fell there. Never had.

The path was rocky. I kept my head down as I walked, watching my step, but as the treehouse drew closer, my gaze seemed to drift up of its own accord, drawn to the tree that housed the wood and glass structure I remembered my dad building when I was a gangly teenager. Back then, I hadn't appreciated the tenacity it took to build something so beautiful, but I was a better man now.

Mostly.

I reached the gnarly staircase and took a deep breath, bracing myself for what I wanted the most—Rami. Then I climbed the steps to the treehouse and slipped inside.

At first glance, my eyes told me Rami wasn't there, but I *felt* him, even before I spotted him hunched over his phone on the old leather futon. "Hey."

His dark gaze found mine. He smiled and the anxiety I couldn't quite unpick by myself lost its sharp edges. "Hey," he said. "Come to kick me out of your dad's office?"

"No, I brought your car back. And it's not my dad's. I was just telling your sister it doesn't technically belong to anyone, except maybe the queen."

"How do you work that out?"

"This land is wild. It's not mine, it's not hers."

"How come this is here then?"

"Best satellite signal. And my dad didn't care about red tape. Besides, no one from the council has been up here since the fifties, so I think you're safe for now."

Rami gave a dry chuckle. "Define 'safe'. Now I'm connected to the matrix again every man and his dog wants a piece of me."

No one wants you as much as I do. "Work?"

"Yeah. Um…" Rami's hot stare doubled down. "I spoke to my boss."

"Your boss?" My voice was scratchy, as if I hadn't spoke for a thousand years. "About what?"

"About working remotely until after Christmas. I mean, I still need to go home and fetch some things so I'm not wearing my sister's clothes all the time, but other than that—"

"You're staying?"

"For a few weeks," he said evenly, what he wasn't saying —*not forever*—laced in every syllable. "Until the day after Boxing Day when my current cases come to an end and I go back to the prison to pick up new ones."

Not forever, not forever, not forever. But still my heart leapt. Christmas was a few weeks away yet, and I was busier than a worker bee selling trees and shipping firewood and timber. But I was home every night with time to spare before the moon took over, and I—

It's not all about you. He has a family who want to spend time with him. A child who needs him. Think about Charlie.

"Fen."

"Hmm?"

Rami was in front of me. He was wearing different clothes to the ones he'd left my house in that morning; a pink T-shirt

—Safia's—and his own jeans. The pink was good against his dark hair and warm skin, *really* good, and I couldn't remember what I'd come up here to talk to him about. Just that I wanted to kiss him and keep him wrapped around me in my bed forever.

I'd never felt like that before. I mean, I'd only slept with people I was in some kind of relationship with, but I'd never felt so consumed by someone as I was by Rami and we hadn't even got that far—in the sexual sense. *And you won't if he leaves.*

Man, my head was a wild place to be right now. Common sense told me that Rami leaving didn't mean he'd never come back, but the thought of weeks, months, *years* passing before I saw him again was...awful.

"Hey." Rami grasped my hands and squeezed them. "Just because I'm sticking around longer than I said I would, doesn't mean I'm expecting you to, like, totally bang me or anything."

A grin split my face. "No?"

"Nah. I wouldn't stop you, but...I heard you when you spoke, and I respect you. You know that, right?"

I did. It wasn't Rami making my head spin on a loop, it was me. And I needed to be honest with him before I combusted. "I'm scared of getting hurt," I said. "I don't do half measures and casual emotions. The way I feel about you, if we fucked I'd probably want to marry you, and I'm not robust enough in here—" I tapped my head—"or here—" I tapped my heart—"to handle rejection."

Rami slid his hands up my arms, then wound his arms around my waist, pressing his face into my neck as he sighed. "I wish I was in a place to give you more. I'm just so caught up with Charlie and I don't know what the hell I'm doing with my life."

I kissed him. And not a peck or a soft brush of lips. A full on lover's kiss that drove him backwards until he hit the wall.

Rami grunted in surprise, but he didn't fight me. Not even a little bit. He kissed me back, fierce and hungry, and yanked me closer, slamming us together.

Fire sluiced through me, and the part of my soul that was led by primal desire let it burn. I slipped my hands beneath that damn pink T-shirt and lost myself in the sensation of his skin against my palms. I swallowed his low, throaty moan, and pressed my dick to his, eyes rolling at the pure, sinful pleasure that heated my blood. God, I loved how he made me feel. It was wicked and wonderful, and the delay in letting him go had given me space to enjoy it.

I could breathe and want him at the same time.

I—

Rami pulled back, panting, cheeks flushed, eyes hooded and dark. "Wow."

"What?"

"Just wow. It's all I've got."

"Sorry."

"For blowing my mind with a fucking kiss? Shut your mouth."

I loved this side of Rami. His shrewd, gentle demeanour at work was what had attracted me to him in the first place—alongside the fact that he was *hot*—but his rougher edges did something to me and I seemed to marvel over it every time we were together, making me glad no one had to listen to my brain constantly repeat itself. "Consider my mouth shut."

"First time for everything."

I grinned.

Rami gripped my jaw and rubbed his thumb over my

cheekbone. Then he sighed. "It's my turn to cook dinner tonight. Are you brave enough to stay?"

"For dinner?"

"No, for a cricket match."

"Sarcasm doesn't become you."

"Yes, it does, or I'd have no sense of humour at all."

A quiet laugh escaped me. Rami had plenty of humour in him, it just so happened that he'd rather laugh at himself than anyone else. "What are you cooking?"

"No idea."

"None at all?"

"Nope. Haven't even looked in the kitchen. I had grand plans, then I got distracted scoping out your dad's office."

"How do you like it?"

"Honestly?"

I nodded. Rami eased out from where I'd trapped him against the wall and stepped to the middle of the room. He spun in a slow circle. "I love it. The Internet strength is better than I have at home. If I'd known this was here all along, I'd have been able to visit more."

"For real?"

"For real. Even without Charlie, it's hard for me to take real time off. I can't remember a time I've been away from my inbox as long as I have the last few days."

"Do you feel better for it?"

"Yes and no."

"Explain."

"Bossy."

I spread my hands and positioned myself against the wall. "You might like it one day."

"Promises, promises." Rami winked. "But to answer your question, I'm enjoying my phone being silent, but I'm angsting about the offenders in my care. Dante Pope was going to ask his brother to spend a day with him at Christmas and not knowing how that turned out is killing me."

I whistled. "Wow. That's progress."

Rami swung his gaze from the window and blazed his red-hot stare my way. "Yeah, well. If you want something enough, you keep trying."

A

I stayed for dinner. And not just because Rami was there, but because I was a greedy sod who never refused a plate of food I hadn't had to cook myself.

And it turned out, Rami was pretty fly in the kitchen. He made a chicken pie with Paddy's home-cured bacon, roast potatoes that were better than my mum's, and because he was my soulmate—*stop it*—baked beans.

I sat next to Addie and helped him eat the stack of potatoes he'd optimistically piled high on his plate—I was good like that. Rami was opposite me, his foot touching mine under the table. We didn't talk much, but it didn't matter. He was *right there*. And he could cook. This day was panning out to be magic.

Safia had Charlie on her lap. He seemed happy enough, but by the time Paddy brought mince pies and ice cream to the table, that little boy wanted the closest thing to a father he had left.

He moved suddenly, climbing over the table to get to Rami and he threw his tiny arms around Rami's neck as if they'd been separated for years, not however long Rami had spent in my dad's treetop office.

Rami chastised him for clambering across the dinner

table, but there was no irritation in the gentle admonishment. Only a deep affection that made my soft heart swell.

I had to look away. It brought my gaze to Safia. I found she was watching them too, and I knew what she was thinking—that this was a bond that could never be broken. She could mother Charlie as much as she liked, he'd always want Rami more. They came as a package now. Where Rami went, so did Charlie, and god, if that wasn't beautiful too.

Eating my body weight in mince pies was my greatest achievement of the day. Addie dared me to eat just one more, but I knew my limits. "I'll go pop," I told him. "Then your mum will have to clean me from the ceiling."

Addie laughed and dragged me away from the table to show me the galaxy model he'd made from some kindling sticks I'd carved into globes for him. "Uncle Rama said he'd help me paint them now he's staying for Christmas."

"That's nice." I spun the model around. It was pretty intricate for a kid so young, but nothing about these kids surprised me anymore. They had Paddy's ability to turn their hand to just about anything and the will to do it right that was apparently a Stone trait, though it had skipped Damon.

"You're coming for Christmas Day, aren't you?" Addie blurted out of nowhere.

On the spot, I took a breath to contemplate my answer, but a voice from the doorway beat me to it.

"Of course he's coming. Unless you have somewhere else to be, dear friend?"

I threw a glance over my shoulder at Safia. "The only place you'd find me otherwise is crying into my wood chipper after the last day at the market."

"So you'll come then? You never gave me an answer last year."

I winced, glad Rami was elsewhere. Last year, I'd been too worn out by the business and consumed by despair to give much thought to a turkey dinner and Christmas crackers. And the years before that, I'd worked at the prison, spending the New Year with my parents instead. They'd passed on now and I'd resigned myself to sleeping through Christmas Day. Or getting drunk by myself, seeing as my sister lived in Australia and I hadn't heard from her in years. A family Christmas with the McCades *and* Rami? Damn. It was the best offer I'd ever had.

Somehow, though, I still found myself unable to give Safia an answer.

I shrugged and she rolled her eyes. "Whatever. Just show up on the day. There'll be plenty of food."

She turned to go. I stood fast and caught her arm, pulling her into a loose hug. "Thank you. I'll let you know, okay? You know you guys mean the world to me."

"You mean the world to us too. All of us."

Her stare turned meaningful. I ignored it and let her go, slipping out of Addie's room and down the hall. I wasn't exactly looking for Rami, but I breathed a sigh of relief when I found him creeping out of Mae's room.

"He likes her better than Addie. Don't know why when all she does is boss him about."

"Same reason you love your sister, I'd imagine."

"Probably. Wanna take a walk?"

I couldn't think of anything I'd rather do that didn't involve all the things that made my head spin.

We found our boots and coats and slipped out of the warmth of Safia and Paddy's home. I knew their property better than Rami, and I led him on a wander that took us to a sheltered ledge close to the top of Christmas Mountain. From there, we could pretty much see the whole world without getting battered by the wind.

Rami was spellbound. "It's so beautiful up here."

The view had nothing on him, but I kept that to myself. If he couldn't tell how I felt about him by the way I gawped at him all the time I was doing it wrong. "It's nice," I said instead.

Rami shot me a scathing glance over his shoulder. "Nice? Wow, you're a tough crowd."

"Not really. A full belly and a cuddle and I'm happy."

"Well, my sister took care of the belly thing, I guess…" Rami stepped back from the ledge and turned to me, opening his arms. It was so easy to step into them and sink into his embrace. Too easy. My body became autonomous again. I wrapped my arms around Rami and held him tight, hiding in his neck, his cinnamon-scented hair tickling my face. Heat pooled everywhere I dared acknowledge, and definitely in the place I was slightly scared of. The thing was, I'd never wanted anyone as much as I wanted Rami. I'd never felt such a deep, primal desire cloud my mind. It was intoxicating. With him this close, I couldn't think or breathe for wanting him.

I could only kiss him.

So I did, and he kissed me back, and just for a moment, it felt like we were the soul survivors of a beautiful apocalypse.

Too soon, though, he pulled back with a rueful grin. "It's too fucking cold for all the filth that goes through my head when you kiss me like that."

"Like what?"

"Like, if we ever did get around to fucking we'd set the world on fire."

It was quite the image. I smirked. "Maybe we will."

"What? Fuck? Or commit planetary arson?"

"Both. I know I said if we slept together I'd probably want to marry you, but I didn't mean literally."

Rami still had his arms around me. He rubbed my back with both hands. "You don't have to keep explaining yourself. It's okay that you didn't want a quick bunk up. More than okay."

"Quick?"

"You know what I mean."

I did. But the weight of too many complicated conversations was getting to me. Rami was fun. I wanted to enjoy that. Wanted to see his dark brows wave up and down as he took the piss out of me. "It would never be *quick*," I said archly. "I'd fuck you all night long."

Something passed through Rami. Not quite a shiver, but my words did something to him, I could tell. "The last time I hooked up, the bloke was in and out of my flat in forty-five minutes. He had to get back to work, and I had to pick up Charlie. I never caught his name, and I never told him mine."

"Fair enough."

"Is it?"

"Course it is. I don't like one-night stands because of me, not because I think no one else should have them."

"Who did you last sleep with? Fuck, I mean, shit. You don't have to tell me that."

"It's okay." And it was. I was just having trouble remembering that anyone had ever come before him. "It was about a year ago. I met someone when I was hawking timber at an expo in Scotland. I slept with him a month later and I regretted it."

"Why?"

"Because it was all he wanted and he was honest about

that, but I liked him, and my stupid self thought that if I fucked him like any other dude he could get off Grindr, he'd like me too."

Rami frowned. "He didn't like you?"

I shrugged. "I never asked. I was in a weird place and not thinking right. It wasn't his fault. And the sex was...okay, I guess. I just feel kind of empty when it happens without all the stuff we talked about, and I hate that feeling. It makes me —" I snapped my mouth shut. I didn't want to talk about that. Not now, not ever. I'd fought too hard to push it away.

But Rami wasn't a man who could be pushed away if he dug his heels in. How many times had I seen him coax the worst pain out of offenders who *needed* to talk, but didn't know how?

So many.

He was still rubbing my back. "Did it make you want to not be here anymore?"

His whisper was deafening.

I nodded with a heavy sigh. "For a little while. And having sex with someone who didn't care much about me didn't make it better."

"It wouldn't. No-strings sex is only fun when you come at it from the right place."

"Like you do?"

"Like I have done, sometimes. When I've used it as a distraction method for shitty things happening in my shitty life, I've just ended up feeling more, well, shitty."

Rami frowned deeper at the word repetition peppering his statement, but it was a comical expression that made his face adorable. I laughed, and he bit my shoulder. "I'm not that funny."

"Not on purpose, maybe."

"Dick."

"Yup. It's not always for you, though, is it? Dick, I mean? You're bi, right? I always got that vibe from you."

Rami nodded. "Pan if we're splitting hairs. I'm down for whoever if I'm attracted to them."

"Even a moody lumberjack with a cacophony of mixed signals?"

"Your signals are just fine. We're attracted to each other, but we like and respect each other too much to fuck around with our beautiful friendship."

"Sarcasm?"

"No. I told you already. I heard you. We don't have to keep talking about it."

I couldn't tell if I was irritating him or not, or if, maybe, he was just bored with talking in circles. Either way, I let it go and kissed him again, letting whatever happen and trusting him—and myself—enough to go with the flow.

We wound up pressed against the side of the mountain, warming our hands on each other's skin, our lips fused together. I wondered if I could come from just kissing him. It sure felt that way, and I loved that, even if it scared me.

I also loved the sensation of his hard dick against my leg. I ached to touch it, squeeze it, and take him in my mouth, but it was too cold for anything like that, and perhaps it was just as well.

For now.

Okay. My brain was having a fine old time tonight, wasn't it? Or maybe it was my cock. Whatever. If and when I ever did bang Rami Stone, I didn't want him to get frostbite for his trouble.

I stopped kissing him and lay my forehead on his. "I should go."

"Busy day tomorrow?"

"Not really. But I don't want to kiss your lips right off your pretty face."

"You're a sweetheart."

"I know. What are *you* doing tomorrow?"

"Going home to get some clothes."

"To Manchester?"

Rami nodded. "I need my laptop too. And some other stuff for work."

"Are you taking Charlie?"

"Nah, I don't want to confuse him."

It was on the tip of my tongue to offer to go with him, but I swallowed it down. If he wanted that, he'd ask. Besides, he'd once told me he could see Strangeways from his kitchen window if he looked hard enough on a clear day and HMP Manchester was the last place on earth I wanted to be.

We walked back to Safia's place. The mood between us was quiet, and I wondered if it was me—it usually was. When I had too much to think about, I forgot how to speak, which I guess made a change from the motormouth I became when I was happy.

Safia's gate came up on us too fast. Rami laid a hand on the bolt and turned to me. "You know you could, uh, stay the night, if you wanted? I promise I won't jump you."

I couldn't promise I wouldn't jump him, though. My head was kind of a mess. "I'd love to, but I'm too riled to be in bed with you right now."

Understanding flared in Rami's dark gaze. Compassion. A camaraderie, perhaps, that I couldn't quite explain. "Fair enough. I'll see you when I get back then? If I'm not with Charlie, I'll be in your dad's treehouse."

"Don't work too hard."

"I'll try. And Fen?"
"Yeah?"
"I don't think we'd make it to the bed."

10

───────

Rami

I was in my bed, *alone*, for all of five minutes before I fumbled my phone from the bedside table and sent Fen a message.

Rami: *is it weird if I ask you to come with me tomorrow?*

It took him a little while to reply. I presumed he was driving home and tried not to picture him texting while navigating the horrible mountain road. *As if he'd be that stupid.* No chance. Fen Hawthorne was gorgeous, sweet, and kind, and more enigmatic than I'd ever imagined for a man who seemed to wear his heart on his sleeve, but he wasn't fucking stupid.

His reply pinged through ten minutes later.

Fen: *not weird*

Rami: *so...you wanna come? can't promise it'll be fun, but I could use the company xx*

Another ten minutes ticked by, then twenty. An hour later, I figured he'd fallen asleep and spent until witching hours contemplating if I'd been a needy idiot to ask him in the first place. We were casually dating. Kind of. Hanging out. *Occasionally*. Kissing. *A lot*. Why would he want to drive to Manchester with me and watch me shove un-ironed clothes into a bag before turning round and driving straight back? Would I do that for him?

Yes.

My answer was swift and absolute. And it shocked me. Charlie had been my priority for so long, it was strange to have someone else taking up space in my brain. Strange and welcome, though I didn't know what to do with it.

I fell asleep ruminating, and dreamt of a world where the life I had now fit perfectly with the lives of every soul I cared about. The location was vague, but smelt of pine trees and my sister's thyme-scented soda bread, and I woke at dawn horny for Fen and hungry for my breakfast. *What is life right now?*

The answer was no clearer when I came back from cooking scrambled eggs and soda bread toast for six people. Charlie was on my hip, gurgling about something. In recent months, frayed by the juggling act I'd been trying to keep up, I might've tuned him out, but I was all ears now, enjoying his innocent company as I got myself ready to leave him for the day. Apparently not worrying about his parents abandoning him in a crack den was life-changing. Who the hell knew?

My phone buzzed as I was flailing around, one-handed, to leave. Focused on Charlie, I ignored it, shoving it into my pocket, and walked out into the misty early morning to the sight of Fen Hawthorne leaning against the bonnet of my car.

I blinked my surprise, my hurried footsteps coming to a stop. Despite my grand plans to drive my car down Christmas Mountain all the way to Manchester and back, I'd somehow forgotten the only reason I could do that was because Fen had got my car fixed and brought it back yesterday. That he hadn't driven home at all. He'd walked. In the dark and the cold. *You're the worst kissing friend.*

Charlie wriggled out of my grip and toddled to where Fen stood, holding his arms up. More surprise hit me. Charlie had taken well to Safia and Paddy being regular fixtures in his day-to-day life, but he never left me willingly to go to them. Never climbed their legs the way he was Fen's right fucking now.

Fen tore his gaze from mine and scooped Charlie up the way he had that first time in his kitchen. He said something that made Charlie laugh—like, *really*, laugh, pure joy and sunshine. *Damn this man. I could really fall for him.*

If I hadn't already.

I pushed the thought out of my crowded mind and closed the distance between us. Fen and Charlie were having a serious conversation about Charlie's plans for the day. It involved mud and pie.

"Don't eat it," Fen said. "It looks like chocolate, but it's not."

Charlie nodded. "I eat pie."

"Don't say I didn't warn you." Fen moved to hand Charlie to me.

I shook my head. I liked seeing them together. They were my two favourite things. *Damn this man.*

The repeat of the thought made me laugh out loud. Fen shot me a questioning glance. I evaded by hiding my face in Charlie's soft hair. Leaving him for the day was proving harder than I'd anticipated.

Perhaps sensing my seesawing emotions, Fen slid an arm around my waist, effectively sandwiching us all in a loose, three-way hug. "There's a winter wonderland fair in

Tassleton next week. We're hawking trees in the car park. You wanna come with the bairn?"

Tassleton was ten miles away. I'd never been there, but I knew it was posh and pretty. I opened my mouth to ask if there'd be doughnuts there, but Charlie cut me off with an excited squeal."

"Yay!"

I was pretty sure he had no clue what he was agreeing to, but his answer was good enough for me. "We'll come. Now, are you going to tell me what you're doing here at the crack of dawn?"

"Getting an early start."

"On what?"

"On our road trip. Sorry I didn't answer your message. I... fell asleep."

My brain twitched at the hesitation. His explanation matched my assumption, but something felt off. There wasn't much scope to get closer to him, but I tried anyway. "Are you all right?"

Fen's gaze flickered. "Of course. Are you?"

I stared hard at him, as if I could sink into his soul through his eyes and see the parts of him he found so difficult to share, but Safia interrupted us before I fell too deep.

She coaxed Charlie from Fen's arms and held him out so I could kiss him goodbye. "You boys be good," she said. "I have a list of things I want if you can track them down." She stuffed a scrap of paper into my back pocket and a handful of cash. "If you get nothing else, though, bring me some stollen? Addie ate all the marzipan in the middle of the night last week and I cannot be arsed to make any more."

"Um...okay?"

Safia rolled her eyes and disappeared with Charlie,

leaving Fen and I alone, together, like we would be all day. A flutter of something stirred in my belly. Excitement? Nerves?

Both seemed most likely. Fen's company was the best I'd ever had, but there was a niggle in my subconscious too, warning me that growing ever closer to him only to leave again in the new year was a bad idea for everyone. Me. Him. Even Charlie.

Dude, it's not a bad idea to be friends with him. He's amazing.

Truth. But I wanted to kiss him. Hold him. Touch him. And Fen didn't do friends with benefits. Whatever we were doing now had to be something more, or sooner or later, he'd pull back, and I wasn't sure I could bear that. *Fuck. What if I can't give him up?*

"Hey." Fen still had his arm around my waist. He held me a little tighter and brushed a soft kiss to my cheek. "I've got an idea."

"Oh yeah?"

"Yeah. How about we spend the day pretending nothing else exists? Just you and me and a road trip."

"To my shitty flat in the city?"

"Doesn't matter where we go, I reckon we just need to stop thinking for a few hours."

It sounded too good to be true, and I didn't know if I was capable of it. My siblings had always made endless fun of my ability to sit in the corner and frown over everything and nothing—even the good stuff—forever. I wasn't sure I could give that up either, but for Fen, I'd fucking try. "Sounds good to me. You ready to go?"

"I'm here, aren't I?"

He was. And bowing to the rules we'd just set in place, I didn't wonder why. I fished my neglected car keys from my pocket and waved them in his face. "Let's roll."

Escaping the mountain with Fen seemed a bigger adventure than it actually was. My heart was thundering like a runaway train before he'd even climbed into my piece-of-shit car with me.

I wondered if his heart was thumping too, considering he was about to endure my terrible driving all the way down the mountain path he didn't trust me to traverse on foot. *In the dark, idiot. It's daylight now.* But still. It was a treacherous road and my car was as temperamental as I was.

At least, it used to be. I turned the key in the ignition and the spluttering groan that usually greeted me was absent.

I shot Fen a dry glance. "Okay, who are you and what have you done with my moody alternator?"

Fen grinned. "They had one lying around at the garage. I swapped it for a six-foot fir and a box of logs."

"You traded my car for a Christmas tree?"

"Yup."

"What about labour costs?"

Fen shrugged. "He owed me a favour."

"And you owe me a bill for the rest of it. And don't even pretend you didn't pay it for me, because I know you did."

He didn't deny it and I glared at him harder before I decided it didn't fucking matter. I'd pay him back when we got to Manchester and we could forget all about it.

I eased my car out of Safia's gate and to the mountain road. Fen kept his gaze on me, but he seemed tense, as if he was forcing himself not to keep tabs on my steering.

Sensing his struggle, I focused on the road, manoeuvring through the narrow twists and turns and trying not to think about the last time I'd driven in the snow and the dark, oblivious to the danger of Christmas Mountain. To the danger I'd put Charlie in.

Despite my best efforts, though, I did think about it, and when we reached the bottom of the fell, Fen rubbed my thigh. "Scared of heights?"

"What do you think?"

"That you're angsting about something you can't change."

He spoke with a smile, a soft one that made his eyes sparkle. I pulled into the lay-by at the bottom of the mountain road and gave in to the urge to touch him.

My fingers tangled in the hair at the nape of his neck, and my forehead found a home pressed to his. "I'm trying to figure out what possessed me to drive up there in the dark with Charlie in the back of the car. Knowing I put him in danger is killing me."

Fen took a breath, slow and deep. My lungs mimicked him of their own accord, as if we were connected on a level that was permanent.

Indelible.

Inevitable.

"You were upset," he whispered. "Desperate, even. And you didn't get all that far. Chances are you'd have come to your senses and driven right back down again anyway."

"What if I hadn't?"

"What if you had?"

"That's a crap argument."

"You can't argue with something that never happened."

I knew that. I dealt with offenders battling anxiety all the time and reasoning them out of theoretical catastrophes was a skill I was proud of. "It was so strange, that night. I've never felt the urge to come here before, but I was on the road before I knew what I was doing, and it wasn't even Safia I was thinking about—it was this place and I don't know why."

"Do you need to know why?"

"No. Yes. Maybe. I don't know. I just—" Fuck. I had no clue what I was trying to say, or where it was coming from. All I knew for sure was that being here, in this moment, with Fen, was everything I needed.

So tell him.

I settled for kissing him.

He kissed me back.

Once.

Twice.

Three times.

But we couldn't stay in a lay-by all day. We had shit to do. Or, rather, *I* did, and I had the hottest wing man ever along for the ride.

I drew back and put the car in gear again. That motion was suspiciously smooth too, but I said nothing. Just absorbed his warm grin and let it heal parts of me I hadn't known were broken. Being with Fen was like that: holistic. He'd always made me feel good. "I missed you," I blurted.

Fen waited for me to turn onto the main road, then he squeezed my thigh again. "When?"

"When you were gone from the prison. I was so fucking gutted something awful happened to you and I didn't know if you were okay. But it wasn't just that. I kept looking for you, hearing your voice when you weren't there. It haunted me."

"I'm sorry."

"No. That's not what I meant. I just need you to know I never stopped thinking about you."

Fen was silent a moment. I gave it to him and kept my eyes on the road. It wasn't a particularly long or complicated drive to Manchester, a couple of hours. Fen liked music—he hummed a lot, tapped his fingers to the beat. I fiddled with the radio while he was lost in thought and Radio 2 blasted through the speakers, Wham! again, because we were just that lucky.

I jabbed my fingers at the buttons, fighting to shut George up.

Fen laughed and took over, making a smooth transition to Magic FM and more fucking Christmas songs.

Band Aid. Fuck my life.

"I like this one," Fen said. "Don't pull that face."

"What face?"

"The one that makes you look like a bulldog chewing a wasp."

"I thought you liked my face?"

"I do."

I tossed him a smile.

He smiled right back, and suddenly Bono bleating through my ancient car stereo didn't seem so annoying.

We made good time. My flat appeared in the distance two hours after we'd left the mountain behind. Anxiety flared in my gut, but somehow I knew it wasn't mine.

I turned to Fen. His face was impassive, but his broad shoulders were tight, jaw set, and a sickening thought occurred to me. "Have you been back here since you left?"

"Here?"

"The city."

He shook his head. "I got airlifted to a hospital in Leeds. When I got out, I paid someone to clear my flat and drive my stuff up north."

"Things were that bad?"

Fen averted his gaze to the window. "I was a mess and

there was no one around here to help me, so I ran home to an empty house and put myself back together there instead. Stupid, right?"

"To seek comfort in the familiar? Sounds pretty sensible to me, and you're not the only one who ran away up a mountain, remember? We literally talked about it a couple of hours ago."

Fen hummed. A week ago, I might've taken the hint to shut my mouth. But we were closer now. Maybe he was ready to talk. "How long were you in hospital?"

"Three weeks."

I took a breath. Three weeks was a long time to be in hospital, but no time at all to turn your back on your entire life.

As if he could sense my thoughts, Fen sighed. "I didn't plan on never coming back. I didn't have my flat cleared until six months later."

"Oh."

We were nearing the block where I lived. I pulled into the car park and into the space allocated to my flat.

Fen was lost in thought again. I shut the engine off. The radio went with it, cloaking us in a silence that seemed to make him jump.

"We're here," I said. "You coming in?"

"Sure."

My flat was on the fourth floor and was as dark and grim as I'd left it.

I opened the blinds—all of them except the kitchen to spare Fen a view of the prison, and myself the contents of my fridge as I emptied it into a bin bag.

Fen busied himself picking up Charlie's toys and rescuing

the dry washing from the airer. "This place is nice," he said. "But it doesn't feel like you."

"I never meant to stay here. It was a stop gap when I came to the city to keep an eye on Damon, but life got away from me."

"Doesn't it always? To everyone, I mean. Not just you." Fen peered at the photographs dotted around my living room. Damon. Safia. Our parents. "Your mum was beautiful."

"Thanks."

"You look like her."

"Double thanks." I held up the bin bag. "Back in a sec."

I jogged downstairs to the wheelie bins and ditched the bag of out-of-date food, thankful my bare shelves had saved me from a horror show that could've been far worse.

Back inside, I found Fen in the kitchen. He'd opened the blind and spotted the prison in the distance.

I didn't stop to think. I came up behind him and hugged him tight. *Fuck. He's shaking.* It was subtle, like everything else that had changed in him since I'd known him before, but I felt it all the same.

And it hurt.

Fen was a good man. The best. He didn't deserve this pain.

I kissed between his shoulder blades, then gently turned him around. "Will you tell me what happened?"

Fen's hands twitched, like he wanted to lay them on me, but didn't trust himself not to squeeze too tight.

Fuck that.

I took his hands. Squeezed them hard enough to bend the bones. "I've got no milk."

"Have you got booze?"

"Probably." I released him to open a few cupboards. A

bottle of cheap vodka I'd confiscated from Damon once upon a time was buried at the back of one.

I passed it to Fen.

He took a healthy swig then poured the rest of it down the sink. "I'll get you another one sometime."

"I don't want it. I want you to be okay."

"I am."

"But you weren't?"

"Not for a while." Fen wiped his mouth on his sleeve and took my hand. "Can we do this somewhere else? I've never liked looking at that place. It's like an evil death castle."

It shouldn't have been funny, but his word choice was golden. A laugh escaped me and I tugged on his hand. "Come on. I'll show you my bedroom."

"Finally. I've only been asking a couple of years."

"Ha ha." I took him to my room. It was remarkably tidy, probably because I'd spent most of the last few months passing out on the couch or sleeping with Charlie.

The bed was made. I sat on the edge and coaxed Fen to do the same, but he went one step further and flopped back, staring at the ceiling.

There were no words for how gorgeous he was splayed out on my bed. God, I wanted to climb on top of him and fucking worship him, but this wasn't the time, more so than ever.

I lay next to him, stretched out on my side, facing him.

Fen didn't look at me, but I felt it when he made the decision to start talking, even though it took a moment for him to take a breath and start.

"I got jumped in the lifer's wing," he said. "I didn't usually spend much time up there, but they were short-staffed, and I took some extra shifts that month."

"Why?"

He shrugged. "Why not? I didn't have much going on down here except work, obsessing over the gym, and living to catch a glimpse of this hot probation officer I happened to know."

"He sounds like a wanker already."

Fen chuckled, but his humour faded as fast as it had arrived. "There was a rookie up there. One of the old-timers was supervising her, but they knocked off on a two-hour tea break. She left a gate open. It wasn't her fault, but someone got through it who shouldn't have and they stabbed me in the neck before anyone realised they were gone."

"Fuck." A shuddery breath escaped me. "How bad was the injury?"

"Bad enough that I nearly bled out in the two hours it took them to get to me. The offender dragged me into his cell and barricaded us inside. I had to lie on the floor and listen to him tell them what he'd do to me if they kicked the door in."

Shock filled me. I'd always known there was more to what had happened to Fen than the horrific details I'd picked up, but a fucking hostage-taking? Damn. No wonder he hadn't come back. "How close was it?"

Fen finally looked at me and he didn't ask me to clarify my question. He *knew* what I was asking him. "I fought him off in the end. Don't know how, I was so far gone with blood loss, and I don't really remember it. All I know is if I'd left it ten minutes longer, I'd have been too dead to haul myself from the floor and clatter him with the kettle. I got a TV in my face for my trouble—" he pointed at a small scar I'd never noticed bisecting his eyebrow—"but it gave them enough time to get in."

After so long knowing the bare minimum, the sudden

influx of details was overwhelming. Perhaps for Fen too. He closed his eyes, his chest rising and falling too fast.

I waited.

When he looked at me again, his eyes were red. "It's the waiting that haunted me. I woke up on that floor every night for six months. It was...messed-up. Your sister and her crazy brood were the only thing I had that made me feel good. Makes sense now I know they're part of you."

"Are you okay now?"

For the first time in what felt like forever, though it had only been an hour or so, Fen smiled. "Most days. It creeps up on me sometimes, but it happens less and less. I'm sorry it took me so long to talk about it, I just—I don't know. Whenever I've had to for the investigation and stuff, it's set me back, and I don't want to be that guy who wallows in the past."

"How far along is the investigation? Do you have to give evidence in person?"

"My GP wrote a letter saying it would cause me serious harm. I wrote a report and read it out on a video link a while back. And I don't care about where it's at or the outcome. You know what the prison system is—whatever happens to Officer Tea Break isn't going to change that."

He was wrong. Maybe. Sometime it took a thousand tiny shifts to move a mountain. But if Fen was okay, nothing else mattered.

We lay quietly for a little while. Fen's breathing slowed. The goosebumps on his arms faded and I wondered if he'd fallen asleep. Stress was like that—it kept you awake for days at a time, or knocked you out as a defence mechanism. I'd always danced the insomniac's dance, but maybe Fen was the opposite.

Either way, I gave him space.

Mental space.

Because I wasn't leaving his side anytime soon.

I let my own eyes droop shut. I didn't doze off, but I definitely left the room.

Gentle hands on my face roused me sometime later.

Fen was closer, leaning over me, gaze intense but lighter than it had been when he'd shut his eyes at the end of his fucking horrible tale. He smiled a little and it was like the glittery sunlight hitting the virgin snow on Christmas Mountain. "Can I kiss you?"

"Why are you asking when you've kissed me a thousand times already?"

"Because it feels different now."

It did. But I couldn't explain it. Couldn't gather the threads of the past few weeks, months, and years and build a tangible map of how we'd got here.

I could only kiss him, so I did, and the moment our lips touched, the fire between us sparked hotter than it had ever been. Fen covered me with his body, his mouth taking mine, his tongue sliding between my lips. He stole my breath. My coherent thought. All I had sluicing through me was *want want want* and I was powerless against it.

I threw a leg over Fen's hip and rolled us, forcing him onto his back, straddling him how I'd pictured when he'd first flopped onto my bed. I ground against him, feeling his hard length against me, the bulge in my own jeans leaving me dizzy.

We kissed again, deeper, fiercer. I slid my hands under Fen's clothes, finding his warm skin, and pressed down on his cock.

He groaned, throaty and raw, and I nearly lost my fucking

head. Then reality caught up with me, and my subconscious put the brakes on. *He doesn't want this, remember? Stop pushing him.*

I pulled back, panting. "Sorry. You make me crazy sometimes, you're so fucking hot."

Fen stared, breathing as hard as me.

Harder.

He took my face in his hands and whispered my name. "Rami?"

"What?"

"I don't want to stop."

Fen

My heart was pounding. Thundering. I barely heard the words as they tumbled out of my mouth. *"I don't want to stop."*

I didn't know how far I'd get before my soft heart got scared, but my soul needed this. I needed *Rami*.

We rolled around on his bed, mouths fused together as we stripped our clothes. Rami moved like I imagined he danced, with grace and poise, his elegant limbs wrapping around me, his back arching into my touch.

I gazed at him, soaking him in as our underwear became the last barrier between us. The heating was off in his flat, but his skin was flushed hot and shiny with a fresh layer of clean sweat. He was so gorgeous I couldn't stand it. I pointed at the black cotton clinging to his sinful hips. "Take them off?"

Rami smirked. "You do it."

Damn.

However this fell, I was gonna be dead by the end of it.

I reached for the boxer briefs hiding his dick from me and

pushed them down his hips and thighs, leaving him to do the rest and kick them away while I drank him in. Man, was there any part of this bloke that wasn't beautiful? I was running out of places to check.

Grinning, Rami shifted closer and shoved at my boxers. "Your turn."

I didn't protest. I let him take them all the way down my legs and sucked in a harsh breath as he came level with my cock. Desire rippled through me, sharper than before. Brighter. I was so hot for him it was hard to imagine the thought process that had told me we shouldn't do this. I didn't regret waiting for this moment, I just didn't...feel it anymore, despite the fact that nothing had changed.

Rami tossed my boxers somewhere and crawled up my body. He rolled onto his back, pulling me over him, and kissed me so hard I bucked my hips, searching out friction.

My cock tangled with his and we both groaned. Inhibitions gone, I reached between us and gripped us both, jacking us together, my eyes rolling at the unreal pleasure firing through my nerves. "You feel so good."

Rami groaned again, licking his lips as his eyes grew hooded. "I knew your big hands would be the fucking death of me."

"Only my hands?"

"I didn't dare think about the rest of you in case the fantasy never came true."

Rami punctuated his words with a kiss, but broke off with another low moan that went straight to my dick, and in that moment, my brain deserted me. I couldn't think, only feel, and Christ if he didn't feel so damn good. I worked us harder, faster, squeezing us together as I revelled in the sensation of his dick sliding against mine.

It was hypnotising. For long minutes, I couldn't look away.

Then the first rush of orgasm hit me and I panicked. *Too soon.* I wasn't ready to stop.

I slowed my hand.

Rumi hummed and pushed me onto my back. I was bigger than him, stronger and heavier, but there was nothing weak about Rami. He restrained me with one hand splayed on my chest while the other reached for my aching cock. "Can I blow you?"

"You don't want to fuck?"

He shook his head. "Not today. I want what you want."

I opened my mouth to protest. To tell him that the connection I'd been waiting on had been there all along, but he silenced me with a kiss and a whisper. "Not yet."

I didn't have the headspace to figure out how I felt about that. Part of me was relieved because maybe, just maybe, Rami was right. But there was another part of me too, a selfish part that was bone-deep scared that we'd never get this moment again and I'd have to live the rest of my life knowing I could've fucked this beautiful man and I didn't.

That part of me was small, though. All I truly wanted was for Rami to be happy. For him to feel good and have no regrets. If that meant a blowjob, I wasn't about to complain.

I nodded and his smirk turned wicked. He moved down my body with his lips, leaving a trail of fire in his wake and seeking out sensitive spots I hadn't known existed. I *trembled* beneath him, as if it was the first time I'd ever been naked with a man, and my breath became short, sharp pants before he'd even taken me in his mouth.

His lips touched my cock with a gentle kiss. I settled a

little. Maybe I could take this. Maybe I could make it through without every part of me combusting.

Then he opened wide and sucked me in, and everything went white.

Pleasure came thick and fast as my dick slid down Rami's throat. He swallowed around me and sucked me hard, reeling me in, only to back off again with teasing licks from root to tip.

It was so good. *Too* good. I fought the feeling, and my hands curled into fists.

Rami pressed his palm against my abdomen and looked up at me. "Relax," he whispered, lips wet and shiny. "This isn't all we have."

How he could read my mind *and* my body so well, I had no idea, but his light touch to my belly was grounding, even as his wicked mouth took me hostage again, his tongue lashing my balls before he swallowed me whole.

My answering groan was inhuman. Primal. Animalistic. I didn't have the brain power to settle on a single descriptor. I didn't have anything except raw heat searing my nerves. Rami wasn't kind to me. He tortured me, and just when I thought I'd combust into flames, he scraped his teeth along my shaft.

I was done. My body bucked from the bed and I came hard down his throat, my harsh yell loud enough to wake the devil. His strong hands on my hips stopped me from jerking us off the bed altogether, and then he was on me, straddling my chest, pumping his dick until he came too, splattering my blistering skin with his release.

He slumped forward. I put my shaking hands on his shoulders, but otherwise, I had nothing. I was a blank page— a blown mind with nothing but laboured breath inside me. I felt...brand new. As if waiting so long to be with him this way had been an act of healing.

Magic blowjobs. Who knew?

Not that I truly thought Rami's mad skills had cured me of anything, but I was loving this moment, and I let myself have it.

Rami got up and cleaned us both off, then he came back to the bed and lay beside me, his chin on my chest. His hair was a mess where I'd tangled my fingers in it, and his smile was sleepy and sated. "We'd be back by lunchtime if we left now, but I don't feel like moving just yet."

Neither did I. It was one of the things I hated most about one-night stands—snatching clothes from the floor and sliding out the door like nothing had happened. "Can we stay a while? I'm loving this too much to give it up just yet."

My words were heavier than the moment, and I got the feeling Rami knew that. But he just smiled and turned his head, laying his cheek over my thudding heartbeat, and tangled together in his Manchester flat, we fell asleep.

12

Rami

In my dreams, we fell asleep on my half-made bed in my Manchester flat, and we woke in Fen's house, cuddled up against the cold fell wind. It was dawn. Charlie was still sleeping, and we had some time to revisit the heady bubble of pleasure we'd found together before life called us home.

The reality was quite different. We came to naked and cold in my unheated flat and realised it was late enough that we had to rush back. Fen had to work, and I'd promised Charlie I'd be home by teatime.

After fudging our way through Safia's shopping list, we zipped home. I dropped Fen at his gate and drove up the mountain under a promise that I wouldn't kill myself on the road, and it was a while before I saw him again.

Two days, in fact. Two *long* days that were full of fun and joy, but somehow seemed empty without him.

I missed him. A fact that didn't go unnoticed by my sister

when Fen finally reappeared in my life and she caught me peeping at him from the kitchen doorway like a weirdo.

"He'd make an amazing stepdad," she whispered in my ear.

I turned to glare at her, but she was already backing away, an impish grin on her pretty face.

"Just saying," she mouthed.

"Fuck off," I mouthed back. It was a wasted effort, though. She was already gone, and even if she'd been at my side, I'd have ignored her in favour of the scene I was creeping on in the kitchen.

Fen was at the table, drawing with all the kids, even baby Lalla who was sleeping peacefully in the crook of his elbow. Charlie was perched on his knee, stabbing a crayon in the vague direction of the actual paper.

Smiling, Fen drew a circle. Charlie scribbled at it with a brown crayon then laughed. "Rama!"

Fen chuckled too. "He's prettier than that. Draw some big ears on him."

From my position unseen in the doorway, I rolled my eyes, but my heart felt so full it made my chest ache, and I didn't know how long I could look at this perfect scene without crying.

Not long, as it happened. Eyes burning, I backed up and fled the house, following the path back the way I'd come to the office in the sky I'd settled into over the last few days. Working from home in a giant treehouse had turned out to be the stuff that dreams were made of. Every morning, I got up with Charlie, made breakfast for him and the other kids, then I handed him to Safia and hiked to the magic tree on the other side of the mountain and spent the morning clearing my inbox and honouring the last few appointments of my current caseload.

Honestly, with the peace and quiet I needed to work, it wasn't a lot, and it left me plenty of time to wonder what I'd made so much fuss about. And, to contemplate my future. As much as I'd protested the idea of giving up my life in Manchester and decamping to a remote mountain for the rest of my days, the arguments I'd relied on were starting to fall flat. Working remotely suited me—more than that, I enjoyed it, and there was nothing to say I couldn't spend a few days a week at the local prison if I stayed in the probation service.

It was that simple. And then there was Charlie. I'd worried he wouldn't settle in a place so far removed from all he'd ever known, but in the short time we'd been here, he'd put on weight, gained a glow to his chubby cheeks, and he no longer woke in the night screaming my name. With Mae for company, he slept like a log, and for three days straight I'd had to wake him up for breakfast. It was a strange existence, brand-new, and yet familiar, and I was growing to love it.

Which led me to my next dilemma: my goddamn heart. Because there was no doubt I'd already lost a large swathe of it to the sweet, hot lumberjack I couldn't stop thinking about. When I wasn't focused on Charlie, Fen owned every thought I couldn't control, and with the scene in the kitchen playing on repeat, I'd now found a way to combine the two.

I was so fucked. I was *obsessed*, and the heady few hours we'd spent in my shitty flat hadn't helped. Work forgotten, I closed my eyes and relived every kiss and snatched breath that we'd shared. Every rush of mind-bending pleasure. I'd never been so hot for someone. I'd never *burned* for someone the way I had that morning in my abandoned bed. Could I walk away from that? Could I give him up? With Charlie and my job off the table as reasons to leave, they were questions I couldn't avoid, and perhaps the answers were what Fen had been afraid of all along.

And I had reason to fear too. Fen and I were great together, but it had only been a few weeks. What if it all went to shit? Life on the mountain was challenging enough without a broken heart.

He'd never break your heart.

But what about him? The heat of our snatched encounter faded away and I pictured the scar on his neck, remembering the deeper, unseen ones he'd talked about. Finally. At least, it felt that way to me. I think. The ache in my chest was hard to decipher. On the one hand, I was relieved that I now knew what had driven Fen from a job he'd loved so much. The puzzle made sense. But I *hated* what I saw. And I was horrified that I'd known so little about it all this time. I was a shit friend. A distracted lover. Fuck, whatever I was to him, he deserved better.

What happened to him wasn't your fault.

No. But maybe I could've fought harder to find him.

Maybe I would've if my own life hadn't grown so complicated.

"You know, if you think too hard your brain breaks."

I opened my eyes. Fen was leaning in the doorway of the treehouse, his cheeks flushed from the cold, his gaze bright with mischief.

The warmth that bloomed in my gut was something else. My smile was as involuntary as the breath in my lungs. "What makes you so sure I was thinking and not taking a nap?"

"You don't nap. You're too diligent. And..." Fen advanced

on me and smoothed the skin between my brows. "You were frowning like an angry bull."

I opened my mouth to protest, but was fast distracted by the paper-wrapped package in his other hand. It smelt like Christmas dinner and my stomach growled. "What's that?"

Fen held the package just out of reach. "Kiss me and I'll tell you."

Now there was a dilemma. I'd missed lunch thanks to stumbling upon Fen and his super-manny session, but I was as hungry for him as I was for whatever deliciousness he clutched in his big hand.

Fuck it. I fisted his flannel shirt and yanked him down, fusing my lips to his and instantly forgetting about my empty belly. The complexities of everything I'd spent the last few days angsting about evaporated and it was just him and me, stoking a flame that eighteen months of silence had failed to smother.

I could kiss him forever. And for the first time, I didn't chase the errant thought away. I let it linger, settle, and carve out a place in my present. I still had a lot to think about, but this part?

Yeah. We had it down.

Still kissing me, Fen pulled me from his father's rickety desk chair and tugged me to the futon. He sat, taking me with him, and straddling him felt so fucking good.

We moved together like flowing water, a slow grind we didn't have to think about, we just *were*. It was hard to believe we'd only been together like this a handful of times, it was so easy. He knew where to put his hands, where to squeeze, where to stroke. He lit me aflame with every touch, and if not for the fact that we had no condoms or lube stashed in the treehouse...actually, no. I wasn't going to ask him to fuck me. I was still mindful of the fact that rushing headlong into that wasn't what he wanted. A blowjob hadn't changed that.

Right?

I had no idea. And I wasn't about to ask. This, right here, was magical, and all I'd ever need.

Fen slid his hands under my clothes, broad palms splaying across my lower back. He nipped my lip, then my neck, rubbing his unshaven jaw over my tingling skin. "I missed you," he breathed. "When are you going to sleep in my bed again?"

"When do you want me to?"

"Tonight. Tomorrow. All of it."

I chuckled, breathless. "I have Charlie."

"Bring him."

"On a...date?"

"Why not? He's my pal."

I knew that. I'd seen it, today and every other time they'd been in the same room. *But*...God, this was hard. Charlie had endured enough loss and upheaval in his short little life. I couldn't let him get close to Fen, or see us together, until I— until *we*—were sure of our path. "Maybe if I left early...I mean, my car's fixed now. I might be able to work it so he never knows I'm gone."

Fen gave me a shrewd look. It was deep and dark, and pierced my soul. "You think I'd treat him any differently if you and me never got our act together enough to make this official?"

"Of course not. I just don't want him to think slumber parties at your place are the norm if it doesn't work out that way." The words were out of me before I could worry they might upset Fen, but as I stared down at him, I saw not hurt in his gaze, but more of the impish good humour he'd brought with him. "What are you grinning at?"

Fen's already immense smile widened. "You said if, not when. That means you're thinking about doing the thing you said you'd never do."

"I never said never."

"Okay. I'm paraphrasing. But you gave me a whole list of reasons why you'd never consider it. Has that changed?"

"The list? Or my stance on it?"

"Don't be cute."

"Why not?"

"Because I want to do things to you that aren't cute."

Fen's expression turned serious. My body temperature amped up a notch and I almost forgot that we were having an actual conversation.

Almost. Fen hooked two fingers under my chin and dared me to hold his gaze. "We don't have to talk about it," he said. "Just know the fact that it's on your mind makes me pretty damn happy."

Happy Fen was something I could live with. His smile was contagious and I grinned back at him, horny and hopeful all rolled into one, a weird combination for me, as most of my recent sexual encounters had happened when I'd been royally pissed off and swamped with despair. It was a sad fact that I'd never smiled through an orgasm.

The thought made me shake my head and laugh.

Confusion glittered in Fen's eyes. "What's so funny?"

"Nothing. I've just never felt all the things before."

"All the things?"

I couldn't explain, not with words, anyway. So I kissed him again, and resumed the slow rhythm that had made my brain so sluggish in the first place.

Fen didn't protest. He let me rile him up, lulling me into a false sense of control. Then he popped the button on my jeans and treated me to a wicked smirk. "Can I make you come?"

"At this point, probably just by looking at me."

Fen laughed. "Know the feeling."

"Good. If this is one-sided, then I'm off."

"I'll get you off, mate."

Of that, I had no doubt, but I was *craving* his release too. The one experience I had of it had blown my tiny mind and I wanted it again, in whatever capacity he was prepared to give it to me.

Apparently reading my mind, Fen unbuttoned his own jeans too, and manoeuvred waistbands and underwear until he had us both where he wanted us: panting, cocks trapped in his saliva-slicked fist. He'd done this in Manchester too, but it felt different this time, as if any nerves he had were gone and all that was left was want and desire.

Or want*on* desire. It all fit.

Fen began to move his hand, working us together, swiping his thumb through the sticky fluid already coating us both. He had mad skills and I was instantly addicted to watching his dick slide against mine. I rolled my hips to match his rhythm. He mirrored me and it was like we were fucking, just without the soul-shattering pressure that came with it. I wanted him to fuck me—god yes—but I wasn't ready. This was all I could take, and not for long.

Release crept up on me, hiding behind a wall of leg-shaking pleasure. By now, I was groaning with every pump and squeeze of Fen's hand, my muscles seizing up, jaw unhinged, but coming still caught me off guard.

Perhaps it was the sheer force of it punching my hips

forward. Or maybe the volume of the startled cry wrenched from my chest. Whatever. I shot all over Fen's hand, coating his dick and mine with my release, and then I got my reward. Fen *moaned*, deep and low. His hips rose from the futon, abs shaking, and with another quiet, masculine grunt, he came too.

I watched every thread of pleasure pass through him, lost in his glazed eyes, slack jaw, and heaving chest. It was beautiful, and so hot I wanted to do it all over again. Shame I didn't have a magic dick. Or was it? Something this good had to be dangerous.

We came down slowly, me slumped against Fen's chest while his hand remained wrapped around us both. It took a while for my surroundings to solidify again, and when they did, a dry laugh escaped me. "Hope your dad isn't looking down on us."

Fen snorted and finally set my cock free. He opened a drawer in a nearby bureau and retrieved a packet of travel tissues. "He didn't believe in all that, so wherever he is, he'll be having a pint and watching the rugby, not keeping tabs on little old me."

"Just as well."

Fen hummed his agreement and cleaned us both up. I felt sleepy again, like I had in the aftermath of the last time we'd been together like this. Contentment washed over me and I stretched out beside him on the futon, my head in his lap, until I remembered the paper-wrapped package on the desk.

Curiosity—and greed—got the better of me. Under Fen's amused gaze, I got up, jeans still undone, and fetched the package. It smelt even better than it had when he'd arrived. "Is this, like, a roast dinner butty or something?"

"Close. I brought you a barm with turkey, cranberry, and

chestnut stuffing. It's from the market I was at this morning and I already ate two."

"Course you have." Couldn't deny I was relieved. It made me feel less bad about unwrapping the overstuffed bread roll and applying it to my face while Fen looked on. "God, that's good."

"I know, right? Paddy loves them so much he made Safia learn how to make the stuffing so he could have it all year round."

"She knows how to make this?"

"Yup."

"Fuck it. I'm never leaving."

Fen said nothing. Just watched me eat with a brooding grin, and it reminded me that he'd never given Safia an answer about spending Christmas Day with us. I was about to ask him when a calendar notification dinged on my laptop.

"Shit." Still chewing, I got up and tapped the screen. I had ten minutes until the scheduled video call would start, but given that it was an offender Fen knew, it was all the more important that he left. And I didn't want him to leave. Not least because I wanted him to see for himself how this particular offender had flourished in the job Fen had found for him. How happy he was. How safe. Whole. It was all Fen had ever wanted for this kid and it killed me that he'd never got to see it.

Trouble was, it wasn't mine to show him. And Fen knew it too. I hadn't moved fast enough. He'd seen the name on the screen.

"Dante Pope, eh?"

I moved to stand in front of my laptop. "You shouldn't have seen that."

"I know." He stood and stretched his arms over his head,

revealing a strip of his bare abdomen. *Lord, kill me now.* "I'm glad he still has you taking care of him, though. He's someone I couldn't forget if I tried."

I had some sympathy with him there. Dante Pope was a compelling character and I was beyond grateful that his story had a happy ending. I just wished Fen could see it for himself, but I'd already told him too much.

Fen closed the distance between us and kissed my cheek. "I need to get back to work anyway. Got a big fell this afternoon."

"A fell on a fell?"

"That's the worst quip I've ever heard."

I grinned. "I try."

"Try harder."

"Okay."

Fen rolled his eyes. "I don't believe you, but whatever. I'll be home tonight. Come find me if you want that sleepover. And I meant it about bringing Charlie."

"I—"

"Shh." Fen tapped his finger to my lips. "I get it. I just wish it was different. Him and you. You and him. I like that package."

He left before I could speak, and it was probably just as well, because I couldn't hear myself think over my stampeding heart.

Fen

I was an idiot. And a selfish one at that. All this time Rami hadn't put pressure on me to sleep with him, and I'd failed to return the favour. *"I like that package."* Translation: don't leave me. Or, how he might've interpreted it: stuff the life you had before you came here. I'm more important.

Oh boy. However I looked at it, I pretty much wanted to die. Or at least, go back in time and shove the words back down my throat. Not because I didn't mean them. But because it hadn't been fair for me to say them. Rami had enough to think about without me being a needy idiot. I'd just...man, I didn't know. What happened in Manchester had changed something in me, as if talking about getting shanked by a serial killer had lifted a burden from my soul. Cheesy? Yup. But it was December, so I let myself have it.

I let myself drift home from work and cook enough dinner for the both of us too, just in case he showed up. And after I took a much needed shower, I found myself in the spare room, scrutinising it like a social worker, trying to decide if it was a safe space for a toddler.

It wasn't. The window was too easy to open and the bed was too high, and it didn't even cross my mind that taking my power saw to the wooden legs and lowering it was a ridiculous thing to do.

The window was an easier fix. I attached a chain to the mechanism, preventing it from being opened more than a few inches unless an adult manually took the chain off. It was a five minute job. Sweeping up the sawdust from the bed legs took longer.

It was late in the evening by the time I accepted Rami wasn't coming. I left my phone downstairs to stop myself staring at it all night and went to bed.

I was a deep sleeper. My mum used to say a bomb could go off beneath me and I wouldn't notice. Fair cop or not, I couldn't say, but when a knocking woke me in the morning, I had no idea how long it had been going on for.

Bleary-eyed, I rolled downstairs and opened my front door expecting one of the lads from the timber farm.

Rami's bright grin seemed like a dream. "Morning."

"Morrrnin," Charlie echoed.

A smile split my face. I took Charlie from Rami without a second thought and settled him on my hip, ruffling his dark hair. "Whatcha doing here, little man?"

Charlie said words that made no sense.

Rami laughed. "We brought you breakfast."

It was on the tip of my tongue to ask why. Then I decided I didn't care. They were here. They had food. What else mattered?

I moved aside, waving Rami in. He stepped through the

door and stooped to unlace his boots while I wrestled Charlie out of his Spiderman coat.

Rami came upright clutching a bag I hadn't noticed when I'd opened the door. "It's not much. Just a bacon omelette and some baked mushrooms. You've got bread, right?"

I nodded, half convinced I was still asleep and dreaming of the hottest bloke I'd ever met showing up on my doorstep with my favourite meal of the day.

Rami ventured closer to me. He kissed Charlie's cheek and then mine, lingering in close proximity so I could soak in his cinnamon scent. I was coming to accept that he smelt like Christmas. I didn't know how it had taken so long for me to figure it out. "Are you even awake yet?" Rami rubbed my arm. "I was worried you might be gone already."

"Nope. Still here."

"I can see that." Rami's dark gaze drilled into me. "Are you okay?"

"Yeah."

"Sure?"

I scrubbed a hand over my face. "Think so. I'm just not with it yet."

"Go sit down then. I'll bring you a plate."

"You're eating too, right? I can't handle you waiting on me."

"Mate, I've never refused a second breakfast in my life."

Rami kissed me again, then disappeared into my kitchen. I tried not to enjoy the sight of it too much and retreated to the living room with Charlie. He remembered which remote worked the TV and sought it out, pointing it at the screen like he was here all the time. *Stop it.* I helped him find the channel he wanted and tried not to disappear into my head.

Like magic, Rami appeared with a plate of heaven. And

he'd lied. It wasn't just an omelette and a couple of mushrooms. There were sausages too, Paddy's festive chipolatas with nutmeg and black pepper. "You're spoiling me," I said absently.

"Bite me," Rami retorted with enough edge to make me look at him. True to his word, he had a plate of his own, though it wasn't quite as loaded as mine.

I speared a sausage on my fork and held it out to Charlie. He giggled and bit the end off.

Rami snorted. "I just spent an hour telling him not to do that."

"Sorry."

"It's okay. I don't know why I was trying to stop him. Sometimes, I think the only parenting I do is parroting the crap my parents ranted about when I was a kid. Like, I don't give a shit if he puts his elbows on the table or holds his knife and fork back to front, but I find myself banging on about it anyway. What's up with that?"

"He didn't come with an instruction manual."

"Neither did you."

I liked that he valued our friendship enough to think he needed one. *Friendship? Really?*

Yes. We were friends, unless Rami decided he wanted something else. Friends who kissed a lot and did, uh, other things. Apparently I was okay with that now. Except, I wasn't. I didn't want to just be Rami's friend. I wanted more. *So ask him for more. He doesn't have to live here for you to be together. Manchester isn't a million miles away.* But it wasn't the distance that worried me. It was what it meant for Rami and Charlie. Whatever life they'd had in the city had led them to my door in the first place and their lost eyes that night haunted me in the moments I wasn't thinking about Rami in a totally different context. Maybe they didn't need me, but they needed Christmas Mountain, I felt it in my bones.

We finished eating and Rami took the plates to the kitchen. I heard him washing up but Charlie came and sat on me before I could get up and bully Rami away from the sink. Charlie curled up in the crook of my arm, his thumb in his mouth. He fell asleep.

At some point, so did I.

A

Rami

I had grand plans of taking Charlie into town to do some Christmas shopping and run some errands I'd been putting off since I'd got here. But the moment I walked into Fen's living room to find Charlie and him both taking the world's sweetest nap, I could do nothing but sink into an armchair and stare.

I'd always had a thing for sleeping men. The few partners I'd had who I'd cared about in some way or other had fascinated me when they'd slept beside me. I'd watched them for hours. But none had captivated me more than Fen, and adding Charlie to the mix was my own slice of Heaven.

I felt another shift in my heart.

I want this.

But what was *this*? Morning naps on a leather chesterfield? Charlie wouldn't be a toddler forever, and then what? What about when he was a sullen teenager who didn't want to live in the middle of nowhere? *It's not the moon. Fen's house has Wi-Fi.*

But no one had said anything about living in Fen's house,

least of all him. I knew he wanted me to stay, but for what? So we could creep up and down a gigantic hill for date nights twice a week?

You're being a dick.

I was. And it faded as fast as it had arrived. My heart knew the practicalities weren't that important. If I stayed and Fen and I were meant to be, we'd make it work. The question was—

Actually, I didn't know what the fucking question was anymore. All I knew for certain was that I was a different man to the one who had driven his broken car up a mountain a month ago. My heart had been closed off then, barricaded by all the hurt Damon had left behind. But Fen…fuck, sweet Fen. He'd toppled the gates just by existing and now I couldn't picture a life without him in it.

As the thought completed, a faint shudder passed through the house. Or maybe it was me. Northern England wasn't exactly known for its earthquakes. Either way, it was over so fast I was sure I'd imagined it until Fen startled awake. "What was that?"

I shrugged, uncurling my legs from beneath me as I watched him handle Charlie like he was made of glass and get up. "The earth moving?"

Unimpressed by my terrible jokes, Fen stepped to the window and peered out over his property, glancing up and down the mountain. Even from behind, I could tell he was frowning.

I slid off the armchair and moulded myself to his broad back. The sensation of his bulk against my chest stole any words I might've said, so I just held him until he sighed and turned around.

"You heard it too, right? I didn't dream it?"

"I don't know what you dreamt, mate. Only that you're a pretty sleeper."

Fen's brows rose. "Pretty?"

"Yup. I couldn't look away."

Fen wound his arms around me and pulled me close. Our bodies fit perfectly together and kissing him just happened, light and sweet, as if the horny monster in me remembered Charlie sleeping on the couch more than my conscious self.

I pulled back, lips tingling, warmth radiating through every part of me. "I thought it was something in my head that rumbled like that."

"An epiphany?"

"Maybe. I'm still trying to decode it."

Fen smiled a little, but his gaze drifted to the window again and there was a tension in his big body that was absent in mine.

I stopped molesting him and rubbed his shoulder. "What's the matter? You think it was something serious?"

Fen sighed. "I'd have heard by now if it was, but I need to go check on my crew. We're felling again today and I'm hoping they didn't send a lorry load of timber rolling down the mountain."

"That's happened before?"

He tossed me a grimace that told me I probably didn't want to know. "I need to check. Wait here for me? If it's not a disaster, maybe we could do something today?"

Taking a breath, I opened my mouth to tell him I had Charlie. Shut it again without speaking. He knew we came as a package. He *liked* it. I was done—for now, at least—trying to convince either one of us that any of it was a bad thing.

I settled for a nod.

Fen threw some outdoor clothes on, stamped into his

boots, and left. The quiet in his wake was somehow shocking. I didn't like it. I rubbed the goosebumps on my arms and eyed Charlie, still sleeping on the couch. Fen had covered him with one of those blankets that smelt of him and Christmas Mountain as if they were a single entity. I crouched and took a deep inhale, not giving a shiny toss if it made me a weirdo.

The scent filled my senses. Made a home for itself somewhere deep within me, which sounded dirtier than I meant it to and brought me to was something else that was throwing me for a loop: the crazy-hot sexual chemistry I shared with Fen. It was off-the-charts good. He only had to look at me and I was hard, and now he'd let me in a little in that respect? God. I didn't know if I'd survive him fucking me. Surely I'd combust before we got to that point.

Stop thinking about sex. He's so much more than that to you.

For once, though, I didn't need the voice of reason in my head to keep me in line. I *knew* what Fen was to me. He was the kindest, sweetest, funniest bloke I'd ever met, who just happened to be *smoking* hot. He was my every fantasy come to life. How did I get so lucky that he seemed to think the same of me?

He came back before I figured it out, still frowning that adorable frown.

I rubbed his arm. "Did you lose any timber?"

"Nope. And no one heard the rumble either. Do you think we imagined it?"

"Both of us?"

"Yeah. I mean, maybe we're so connected we have the same dreams."

He was taking the piss, and I'd been awake at the time of whatever the hell we'd both heard, but I liked the sentiment.

It made my stomach flutter and my chest feel warm. "Works for me." I kissed his cheek. "Maybe it was Charlie, though. That little git has farted me into oblivion more times than I can count."

Fen laughed loud enough to wake Charlie up, but it wasn't with a jump, it was with a smile, and he slid from the couch and toddled into Fen's arms.

Grinning, Fen lifted him, holding him between us like our most precious thing.

Charlie poked me. "What doing?"

"Something with Fen," I answered. "I don't know what yet."

"We could go to the fair in Tassleton," Fen said. "Take Addie and Mae too."

"That's how you want to spend your day off?"

"It's not my day off. I need to check on the stalls there— we have two, one at each end. And I promised your sister I'd get her some goose fat from the Wobbly Bottom Farm stall while I was there."

"What does she need goose fat for?"

"Christmas Day potatoes."

I'd had two breakfasts, but my mouth watered all the same. "If you're helping Safia load her pantry, does that mean you're coming for dinner?"

Fen shrugged. That was it. His full and complete answer.

I kind of wanted to punch him, but I wanted to spend the day with him and the kids more. And I knew full well my fist would bounce off his solid mass and have no impact whatsoever, so it was a wasted effort all round. "Anyone ever tell you that you're a stubborn motherfucker?"

"No."

"Liar."

"Am I?"

I rolled my eyes and texted my sister. Needless to say she accepted our offer to take her oldest monsters off her hands for the rest of day and pretty much tossed them down the mountain to join us.

We loaded them into Fen's car, three kids in the back and us in the front.

I forgot myself and kissed Fen's cheek as he turned in his seat to reverse through his gate.

The kids didn't blink, and neither did he.

14

Fen

I felt like Dick Van Dyke in *Chitty Chitty Bang Bang* with all the kids bundled in the back of my car and it wasn't a bad feeling. Rami was pretty scrumptious too, and I found myself whistling the accompanying song.

Rami rolled his eyes. "Didn't have you pegged for a lover of musicals."

"I can love anything that makes me feel good."

"Oh yeah?"

"Yeah. And this, right here, is nostalgia. We watched that film every Boxing Day when I was a kid. My dad even had an old car like that lying around for a while."

"What happened to it?"

I shrugged. "Sold it to a furniture maker down south. He sent me a chair made with the wooden panelling from the old dash. It's up at the main house."

Rami absorbed that in the quiet way I'd seen him adopt with troubled inmates. That *knowing* way. Because he was perceptive enough to sense there was more going on than the words he heard. But he was wrong this time.

Probably.

Maybe.

"Can I ask you something?" he said after a while.

I glanced back at the kids. Addie was playing with the Rubik's cube he'd brought with him. Mae was chattering poor Charlie's ear off. "You can ask me anything any time you like."

"Noted." Rami shot me a filthy smirk before his expression turned serious again. "Why don't you live in the main house where you grew up?"

"You've answered your own question there."

"Have I?"

I took a tight right turn then nodded. "I *grew up*. I stayed there for a bit when I first came back here, but even with the seasonal guys for company, I was too lonely there, and I heard and saw my parents around every corner, you know? It was like stepping back in time without the good bits."

"That makes sense."

"Good, because I've never said it out loud before. I've never told your sister that her habit of banging on my door every week kept me going when I wanted to drink myself to death either. Do you think I should?"

Rami's eyes widened a touch. Clearly, he hadn't expected me to be so transparent, and I didn't like that. I wanted him to know he could talk to me and get something real.

I wanted to take his hand too, but as we approached Tassleton, the traffic thickened enough to require my full attention.

Thankfully, I had a trader ticket that allowed me to bypass the worst of it and park among the huge vans and trucks that had been in situ all week long. Addie and Mae didn't bat an eye—I had bigger vehicles on the timber farm— but Charlie's face was the cutest picture. I carried him to a tall red lorry with a teacup painted on the side. "You want to go on some rides?"

Excitement vibrated through his tiny limbs. He bounced in my arms as Rami looked on. "Yeah yeah!"

"Come on then."

We took the kids around the fun fair. Rami didn't care for being flung around on the teacups or the pirate ship only Addie was big enough to go on, so I bought him a bag of doughnuts while I rode the brightly coloured rides. It was fun. Heart-warming fun. The very best kind. And when we regrouped and I saw the sugar on Rami's lips?

Yeah. That warmed me too.

I didn't want to go to work. In that moment, there was nothing I cared less about than revenue and transport damage.

But...life wasn't about getting what I wanted and screw everything else. People depended on me to pay their bills and support their families, so I left the man I was pretty close to falling in love with and inserted myself into the bustling trade my team had struck up around the fair.

Business was good. It was a far cry from the days when rabbits had eaten my father's first young firs. I hauled trees, tied nets, and bought lunch for my team. Last year, I'd stayed with them for three days straight, but the truth was, they didn't need my help, and there was somewhere else I wanted to be.

After a pit stop at the Wobbly Bottom Farm stall, I followed the call in my heart to the grotto where an old family friend was still playing Father Christmas thirty years after he'd lost an ale-driven bet with my dad that he didn't have the balls.

Rami was in the queue with the standard expression of a bloke who'd spent a few hours alone with three kids. "I need more doughnuts."

"Is that a euphemism?"

"If you like. Regardless, I'm gonna collect."

Interesting. But first...Father Christmas. Rami took Charlie in while I waited outside with the other two who were too unruly to go in together. He came back for Addie, and then Mae. But she didn't want to go.

"Not without you." She tugged on my arm. "Uncle Rama doesn't even believe in Father Christmas."

I coughed to cover a snort of laughter. "No?"

Rami winced. "She caught me at a bad moment. Take her if you like. I'm about Christmassed out anyway."

I could believe that. Rami was an amazing parent, but it wasn't hard to see that a full-on day with multiple sprogs to take care of was wearing on him.

Mae corralled me into the grotto. She sat on Father Christmas's knee and rudely yanked on his beard. "Did you buy this from the shop?"

Dear Lord. And there'd been me thinking Rami was tired. The git. He'd known this would happen.

Mae was a nightmare. By the time we left the grotto I was pretty sure Old Man Denny was regretting his life choices and wishing he'd never met my dad. He was certainly wishing he'd never met Mae McCade.

Rami's grin was rakish and evil. "Have fun?"

I ran a hand through my hair, resisting the urge to give him an uncharacteristic middle finger. "It was...an experience. But you knew it would be, right?"

There was no contrition in his face at all as he nodded. "She'd already told me she was going to ask him specific details about his sleigh and the star coordinates of planet Earth and the North Pole."

"Did she tell you she was going to pull his beard off and call him Dennis?"

"Erm…"

I grabbed his hand and pulled him close, brushing my lips over his ear. "I'm going to collect too, and it's not going to be a bag of doughnuts."

Rami sucked in a breath, but I backed off before he could reply. The images going through my brain weren't age-appropriate, and I needed to cool off.

Maybe he did too. He didn't look at me for a while. We bought the kids hot dogs for lunch and ate them in front of the brass band playing Christmas carols. Charlie fell asleep, his head lolled on Rami's shoulder while Addie leant against his legs. Even Mae was quiet, her cheek pressed against my belly as she watched the band play.

It was as close to a perfect moment as I'd ever had and I soaked it in until I noticed Mae staring up at me.

Crouching, I held her small hands in mine. "What is it?"

"I don't want them to go," she whispered.

"Who?"

"Uncle Rama and Charlie. Mummo keeps telling us not to get too excited because they're going home after Christmas, but I don't want them to."

I stole a glance at Rami, but he wasn't looking at us. In truth, he seemed half asleep himself, and damn if that wasn't ten shades of adorable. I felt Mae's words too deeply to enjoy it, though.

With a sigh, I turned back to her. "I don't want them to go either."

Mae nodded. "Because you love Rama."

"Excuse me?"

"You love Rama," she repeated. "And Mummo thinks he loves you too. I heard her say it, so why does he still want to go?"

I had no answer to that, save wet eyes and a burning chest, so I smiled instead, and pinched her cheeks until her frown turned upside down. "Rami has to do what's best for him and Charlie and we'll love them both forever no matter what that is, won't we?"

"Of course, dummy. I'm not silly. I don't think that man in there is Father Christmas, *and* I know how to make Daddy's tractor move backwards."

Well, okay then. I wasn't cut out for conversations with tiny perceptive humans, but I wasn't mad about it. How could I be when she'd seen through me so entirely?

I love him.

It should've been a revelation, but it wasn't. How I felt wasn't new. Rami had been on my mind since the day I'd met him, and the last month or so had cemented what I'd already known—that he was everything for me, if only life would give us a chance.

"Fen?"

"Hmm?" I came back to the present to find Rami had replaced Mae. His arm was around my waist, fingers burrowed beneath my clothes stroking bare skin. "Sorry. What?"

"It's time to go," he murmured. "Where did you go? Anywhere nice?"

I smiled at the repetition of a phrase we'd bantered before. "Maybe. I'll tell you later?"

"Sounds like a promise."

"If you want it to be."

Rami's eyes blazed, but we had too many little people around us to finish the conversation. *Tired* little people. We hustled them back to the car and strapped them in. Rami offered to drive home, but I shook my head. I—I liked the ritual of driving him and kids. It felt right, as if it was a dynamic that was meant to be.

At the top of Christmas Mountain, Safia met us at the gate. "Don't even think of driving straight back down this fell," she told me. "Paddy's made a roast, and I need you to test the latest mince pie batch for me."

Put like that, how could I refuse? As if I even wanted to. Rowdy McCade family dinners had been one of my favourite places to be long before Rami had washed up on Christmas Mountain.

I couldn't deny that having him by my side, his hand in mine as we let the kids run ahead to the house, was seven shades of awesome, though. The sense of borrowed time seemed far away, and I could almost pretend this was my actual life. Right here. Right now.

Forever.

Wowzers. I couldn't deal with that image in my head. It was too much, and yet nowhere near enough.

Rami squeezed my hand. "Are you okay?"

I felt like he'd asked me that already, but I couldn't remember what I'd said in response. I smiled. "Of course."

Rami nodded and scanned the horizon for Charlie while I admired his profile, because it didn't matter where my head was at or how my thoughts landed, one thing never changed: this man was beautiful.

Dinner was louder and more chaotic than any other I'd ever lived through at Safia's kitchen table. Addie and Mae fought and screamed. Charlie cried. Rami comforted him, all the while laughing at Paddy's best impression of The Hulk and my retelling of the horrors Mae had put me through in Santa's grotto.

Safia winced and passed me more mince pies. "I'm sorry. She takes after her grandmother. Paternal, obviously."

Paddy launched a badly aimed cream cracker across the table.

Rami caught it with a snap of his hand before it could hit me square in the side of the head. The expression on his face was murder and I wanted him so much in that moment I had to look away and keep my gaze to myself for a solid ten minutes. Did I like his smile more? Sure. But ragey Rami was scorching hot too.

Damn. When had we shifted into the heady space where I couldn't think about him without sex being the dominating theme? Had it always been like this, but I'd been too scared of losing him to notice?

Was I still scared?

Back when I'd met him, I'd understood myself well enough to know the answer to those questions, but pain and trauma had made my brain a complicated place to be. There were people out there who'd suffered far worse than me—I *knew* that. I'd seen it. But that didn't fix the part of me that had been broken. Only time could do that. And love.

Lots of love, in any form I could get it.

Sex was part of that...right?

"Earth to Uncle Fen." Mae giggled and smooshed a mince pie in my face.

Safia opened her mouth to go postal on her, but I laughed, cutting her off, and smooshed a pie right back on Mae's dark head. "Don't try me, kid. I'm the biggest clown you'll ever know."

"You're a sleepy clown," Mae retorted. "So you should stay for a slumber party with Uncle Rama."

I blinked. "Huh?"

The whole table laughed, even Charlie, though his cute bemusement gave away that he had no clue why I was the current source of Stone/McCade amusement.

I didn't have much idea either. I looked to Rami for help.

He smirked and tipped the last of his beer down his throat.

Addie was my last hope. "What did I miss?"

He shrugged. "Mummo thinks you should sleepover with Uncle Rama and I do too. You laugh more when you're together."

A truck of emotions hit my chest, all of them good. A smile split my face in half, perhaps validating Addie's words, and I didn't care. Being with Rami—and Charlie—did make me smile, and I was glad that they knew it. They loved him, and...

So did I.

I wasn't about to invite myself to sleep in his bed, mind. "While I'd love a slumber party with Uncle Rama, I've got a haulage run tomorrow. I doubt he wants me waking him up at four in the morning when I have to leave."

"I don't mind." Rami spoke for what felt like the first time in hours. He trailed a finger up the neck of his empty beer bottle. "Can't deny I'm a grumpy bastard in the mornings, but

I'm still getting used to Charlie being a mountain sloth, so I'll likely be awake anyway."

Safia kissed her teeth. "That's the only reason you can think of to have a lumberjack in your bed?"

"Shh." Rami waved her off. "Don't pull at *that* thread, sister. You don't know me like that."

She didn't know me like that either. No one did.

But I wanted Rami to.

The conversation moved on without me answering the question any more than I had the open invitation to Christmas dinner. But this was different. It was unspoken, but everyone knew I was staying, even me.

Rami and I washed up in companionable silence, side by side at the sink, his hip digging into mine as he dried dishes with an absent smirk.

I wondered what he was thinking, but was swiftly distracted by my own wandering thoughts. He'd slept in my bed already, but something—everything—about this felt like unchartered territory. Even my tingling skin from his close proximity had amped up a notch. Was I ready for whatever tonight would bring?

Was he?

Because I got the impression Rami thought I was a little innocent.

Bless him.

"Get out of your head."

I emptied the sink and wiped my hands on a tea towel. "Why?"

"Because I want you right here."

I turned to him, leaning against the sink. "Oh yeah?"

"Yeah." He didn't elaborate. Just sauntered off to stack

Safia's baking trays on the high wooden shelves made from sliced up railway sleepers.

I was caught in the sway of his hips and the elegant arch in his lean body as he stretched to put the trays away. So often, I found myself drowning in his dark gaze that I forgot how good he looked from behind. His neck, his shoulders, his back. I wanted to touch every part of him. Taste him.

Fuck him.

Startled, I shivered, desire coursing through me with a healthy dose of...something else. Fear? *No.* Not anymore. I wanted Rami and I wasn't scared of what that meant. Sure, there was still a possibility he'd pack Charlie up and go home, but that no longer felt like the end of the world.

He won't hurt me.

And I'd never hurt him.

I couldn't.

Rami came back to me. He barged into my personal space and took my mouth, apparently not caring that his entire family was in the next room. "Charlie's asleep," he whispered when he was done kissing me senseless. "And I want to go to bed too. Come with me?"

I had no verbal answer. Just a nod and an outstretched hand.

Rami took it and led me outside and across the yard to the log cabin where he slept. It was warm and cosy, a thick rug laid out in front of the wood stove that someone had already lit.

"Paddy," Rami said. "He's obsessed with keeping everyone warm."

"I know. I keep him in logs."

Rami laughed and hung his coat on the back of the door. Locked it.

Shut the blinds.

My heart skipped a delicious beat. I unlaced my boots and set them by Rami's, trying not to think too hard about how much I liked the sight of them together, or how sweet it would be to see Charlie's tiny wellies alongside them. I tried not to think at all, and as Rami returned to where I stood by the fire, it got easier.

He put his hands on my chest and the drumbeat of mutual attraction thrummed between us, a deep tattoo pulsating in my blood. "I want to be naked in front of the fire with you. Is that okay?"

"I've heard worse suggestions."

"Good." Rami unbuttoned my shirt and pushed it off my shoulders. Beneath it, I wore a T-shirt with the timber farm's logo on it. Rami pulled it over my head and unbuttoned my jeans.

I smirked. "You're gonna be naked too, right?"

"All in good time."

Rami stripped me bare and sank to his knees in front of me, taking my cock into his mouth so deep it knocked me off-balance.

"Jesus."

He hummed and worked me with a slow rhythm that had me on a knife edge before he'd taken his socks off.

Git. But I let it happen, for a little while, at least. I had grand plans for him, but I was human, and the wicked pleasure of his mouth on my dick was too good to pass up. I let him have at it until I was fairly sure I'd combust if he kept going, then I reclaimed my cock and joined him on the floor. "Lie down."

Watching me through hooded eyes, he lay back on the rug in front of the fire, and I set to work undressing him, working through the T-shirt and joggers combo he'd put on after he'd taken a shower before dinner.

New thing I'd learned today: Rami with shower-damp hair and water on his skin turned me on almost as much as having him naked beneath me in front of a roaring fire.

Something I'd always known: that having his cock in my mouth would destroy me in the very best way. His taste, his scent. The low groan he made as his cock hit the back of my throat. Man, it was everything, and I could've done it all night if my body hadn't cried out for something more.

I pulled back and wiped my mouth.

Rami's gaze was electric. "How far do you wanna go?"

"Depends."

"On?"

"On what you have in your bedside table."

"There's a wash bag in the top drawer."

I got up and padded to the bed. Everything we needed was exactly where he'd said it would be, and I took it back to the rug by the fire. Part of me wondered if we should move to the bed, but Rami was so beautiful like this I pushed the thought from my mind. "Roll over."

Rami's brow twitched, as if he was fighting a grin. For the second time that night, he did as he was told, but I got the feeling he was on his best behaviour. That if we did this again and again and again like I wanted to, I'd have a harder time manoeuvring him.

Fresh heat flooded me. God, could I handle it?

Could I handle him?

I was about to find out.

Nudging Rami's legs apart, I knelt between them and lowered my mouth to his crease. He gasped in surprise, then moaned as I drove my tongue into him, his hips jumping from the rug.

I held him down and brought him to the brink, revelling in his shaky thighs and sweat-dampened skin. It had been a long time since I'd been this intimate with a man, and I'd forgotten how much I enjoyed it. And this was Rami, so everything was a billion degrees hotter. Deeper. It meant more. I was so hard I honestly thought I might die if I didn't get inside him soon.

Again, I pulled back, breathless. "I never asked you if you were okay with me fucking you."

Rami rose on his balled-up fists, his back muscles flexing as he turned his head to look at me. "Is this you confessing to being a diehard top? Cos I don't want to burst your bubble, but I kind of figured."

"How?"

"Gut feeling. And it's fine. I like it all, but every time I've thought about us reaching this point—which is a lot, by the way—you've always been fucking me, and I don't think I could live with anything else right now."

I love you. I pursed my lips together and reached for the lube and condoms I'd brought back from my bedside table raid. My heart thumped as I slid the condom on and lubed up, and I couldn't take my eyes off Rami.

He watched me, his molten gaze tracking my movements. If he was nervous, it didn't show. The only emotion I saw in him was *want.*

As in, he wanted *me*, and I wasn't going to keep him waiting.

He stayed on his hands and knees as I bore down on him, bringing my dick to where my tongue had already been. I slid inside, inch by inch, and his answering groan with every gentle push went straight to my balls.

I fucked him slowly, giving him time he might not have needed to adjust to me, because *damn*, I needed that time too. He was so tight and hot I couldn't take the searing pressure— if I went too hard too fast, it would be over before we'd got started.

Gritting my teeth, I thrust inside him, finding a cadence I could handle. Rami pressed back against me, silently asking for more, but I wasn't there. *Not yet. Please not yet.*

But it was him saying please that drove me on. Him saying my name in a throaty growl.

"Harder, Fen. Please. Fuck me harder."

I couldn't refuse him.

Grunting, I pushed him down, flattening his chest to the thick rug beneath us, and fucked him a little faster, curving my body with every thrust, sweat beading my skin.

Rami gasped, and an unholy moan escaped me. I wanted to screw him all night long, but every sound he made pushed me closer to an edge I couldn't come back from.

It was so good it scared me.

And then it didn't. Something clicked in my soul and I didn't care if this was over in ten minutes. I was so hot for him there was *no way* we were only doing this once.

The thought of fucking him again sent my pulse into the stratosphere. Instinct took over, the primal kind that sent my hands to his waist to hold him tight and punched my hips forward. Harder. Faster. My thighs slapped Rami's heated skin over and over. He shunted along the rug, and I chased him down, digging every harsh growl from him. Every snatched groan.

For long minutes, I had it—a grip on the pleasure

sluicing through me. Then Rami fought his way up and pushed back against me, matching my rhythm, and I lost my head.

What happened next was a blur of the best kind. I stopped thinking. Where we were now and where we'd be tomorrow ceased to matter and it was just him and me, together, like this.

My legs started to shake, and the tremor spread to every part of my body, a tightly wound band ready to snap. Beautiful tension gripped me. I scrabbled for grip on Rami, but it eluded me and I fell forward, moulding my chest to his back.

We were one.

I steadied myself with an arm threaded around his ribcage and reached for his cock with my other hand.

It was hard and waiting, pulsing in my palm.

"Fuck." Rami hung his head. "I'm gonna come."

As the words left his mouth, his back arched and his muscles jumped. Hot fluid coated my hand and he made a strangled noise, shoving me off the precipice I'd been clinging to since I'd slid inside him.

I came so hard I saw stars, burying myself so deep inside him I couldn't fathom how we'd ever be two separate souls again. I didn't *want* to fathom it—I didn't want us to be apart. Not now, not ever.

It was hardly a new realisation, but combined with the ecstasy in my veins, it was as close to magic as sex had ever been for me.

Panting, I clung to him, face pressed into his neck, breathing him in with every heave of my lungs.

I was still shaking. Or maybe it was him. It didn't matter. This was what I'd been waiting for. A soul-shattering connection that lifted the attraction we'd always shared to heights we'd never come down from.

Tell him.

But I didn't need to.

He already knew.

Rami pulled himself together with deep, shuddering breaths. I slipped out of him and disposed of the condom, and I turned back to his open arms.

He hugged me tight. "You motherfucker," he rasped.

"What?"

"You fucking knew the longer we waited the hotter the fire, didn't you?"

"Guilty. It was more than that, though. I meant everything I said about needing a connection with someone to sleep with them."

"I know that. I just had no clue the result would be as mind-blowing as this. Thank you, you've fucking schooled me here."

He was thanking me for caring about him so much I felt his body clamped around mine in every facet of my soul? Okay. It was better than a kick in the nuts. I kissed him long and slow, letting the lingering heat between us creep up again, warming me from the inside out. There was so much I wanted to say, but words didn't come. Only want. Because as rough as we'd gone at each other, the fire that had blown his mind was far from out.

I pulled back and glanced between us. Despite the back-arching climax he'd just had, Rami was still hard.

He smirked. "Guess I'm not done yet.

I smirked right back. "Good. Because I'm not done with you either."

15

Rami

It was like a dam had broken. After weeks and weeks of dancing around the fact that we wanted to fuck each other's brains out, now we were doing it, we couldn't stop.

Like, at all.

We fucked all night, christening the log cabin in ways sweet Paddy had probably never imagined when he'd built it with his bare hands, and I had zero regrets.

In bed, I climbed on top of Fen, straddling him as I slid down his dick again. I was sore and tired, but nothing registered except the blinding pleasure of having him inside me. Of watching him come apart as I rode him.

After, we lay together panting, and covered in sweat and lube and come. Something rose in me, from a happy place I didn't recognise as mine. A surging warmth that I couldn't deny any longer. *Fuck, I'm in love with this man.* I turned to tell him, to let every ounce of feeling I had for him spill out of me.

But Fen was asleep, sprawled on his stomach with his arm flung over my belly and there was nothing and no one that could've made me disturb him.

A sense of peace settled over me. I stroked his face, letting my fingers trail over his cheekbone and into his short beard. I'd tell him in the morning. After all, if I followed my gut and didn't chicken out, we had all the time in the world.

I passed out, falling into the kind of sleep that was like a trip to another dimension. It sucked me in, my dreams of Fen's strong arms around me so vivid it was hard to believe I would wake to that exact reality.

But I did believe it, and more fool me.

Because I woke alone.

Frowning, I sat up, already questioning my sanity. Was it possible to dream the best sex I'd ever had as many times as we'd done it? The answer wasn't clear until my sleep-heavy gaze fell on a note crumpled beside me.

Rami,

I didn't want to leave.

I'll find you as soon as I'm back.

Don't forget me ;)

As if I could forget him. I folded the note and set it on the bedside table. I already felt bereft without him, but I felt good too. Better than good, I felt whole. As though the epiphany I'd been struck with before I'd fallen asleep was all I'd ever needed.

Smiling, I got up and hauled my exhausted body to the teeny tiny shower Paddy had somehow crammed into the log cabin. My grin widened when I found the floor wet and a damp towel draped over the door. Knowing that Fen had been in there while I'd been sleeping off our wild night made me all kinds of happy, and I washed the sweat from my skin without the usual grouch I woke up with.

When I was dressed, I picked my way across the yard to the house. Charlie was still asleep—lazy git—but Safia was awake, nursing Lalla in the kitchen.

"I thought you'd weaned her," I commented, my mind on Fen.

"I did, but I still feed her like this in the morning. She's my last baby, so I'm not quite ready to stop."

"You said Mae was your last."

"And she should've been, the little demon, but life happens sometimes, you know?"

I gave her a dry look and filled the kettle at the sink before slinging it onto the stove. My back was to her while I brewed tea, but I felt her gaze drilling holes in me the way only she could. "What?" I said without turning round.

"Nothing."

"Bollocks. Whatever it is, just say it."

"Why are you so monumentally stupid?"

I snorted out a laugh. It was the Stone way to be sledgehammer-blunt, but my sister had always pushed it the furthest. "In what sense? Or is it a general thing?"

"It's an emotional thing. Fen loves you, and I think you love him, so why are you still entertaining the idea of going back to Manchester after Christmas?"

"I live in Manchester. You think I can uproot like that because I'm dating someone?"

"Dating?"

Okay, it was the worst word choice in the world, and I agreed with everything Safia was saying one hundred percent, but winding her up was too much fun. "What else would you call it?"

A loud crack of thunder seemed to come from her angry soul. As lightning flashed in the murky dawn sky outside, she narrowed her eyes, lips thinning to a glower. "I'd call it a fucking love story if you weren't such a dickhead."

"Don't swear like that when you're holding the baby."

"Don't you dare tell me how to—"

"All right, all right." I raised my hands in surrender before she truly blew her top. "I'm messing with you. You're right, okay? You're *right*. I do love Fen and I'm pretty sure he loves me."

The fury in Safia's gaze evaporated, replaced by a cautious hope that made me feel like the arsehole she thought I was. "And?" she said with a wince. "What about the rest of it?"

"What about it? If I stay here, it's because it's the best thing for Charlie. Nothing is more important than that, not even Fen."

"He knows that. I wasn't messing with you when I said he'd make an amazing stepdad."

"I know. And you were right, but that doesn't mean he wants that. Being fond of a cute kid and being a full-time parent aren't the same thing. I learnt that the hard way."

"What else have you learnt the hard way?"

"What do you mean?"

Safia finished nursing Lalla and set her to sleep in a nearby bouncer. "I mean you two have lost each other once. Are you really going to let that happen again when fate has worked so damn hard to bring you together?"

It would've been so easy to yank her chain all morning, but I was done pretending I wasn't ready to go all in on whatever Fen and I had. He was good for Charlie, and good for me. Add in this crazy fucking mountain and all that came with it and there wasn't much more I could ask for.

I pushed the kettle to the back of the stove, away from little hands and clumsy adult elbows. Then I turned to my sister and gripped her shoulders, holding her in place. "I'm staying. I don't know how it's going to work yet, and I haven't told Fen, but I'm putting my notice in at the probation service today and getting to work on setting up a remote counselling business from the office in the sky."

Silence. Safia blinked as if she'd misheard me. "You're staying? Both of you? Charlie as well?"

"No," I deadpanned, "I'm putting him in a taxi and sending him down south by himself. Of course he's staying too. I mean, it could get complicated if Leanne comes back and—"

Safia cut me off with a loud whoop. She jumped at me, throwing her arms around my neck, and squeezed every ounce of breath from my lungs. "If Charlie's mum wants to be in his life, we'll make that happen, I promise. But we can do it from here, from our *home*, right? You'll get full custody, won't you?"

I nodded. "It's a formality at this point. It was me holding it up in the first place. Monumentally stupid, remember?"

"Fuck off. You were trying to do right by someone who didn't deserve it, and it's time to take care of yourself—and Charlie—by being with your family and that six-foot-four lumber-sexual who wants to give you his giant heart."

It was a lot to take in from one sentence, but I appreciated the sentiment. I grinned at Safia, and as torrential rain thundered down on the roof above us, she beamed right back. "It doesn't matter if you live here or with Fen, we'll *make it* work," she whispered.

"I know."

"You said you hadn't told him you're staying. Have you at least told him you're in love with him?"

I winced. "Not exactly. He was gone when I woke up."

"From banging all night long?"

"Something like that."

"Tell him now."

"What?"

"Tell him *now*." Safia punctuated the repetition with a gentle shove.

"He's not here. He left on that haulage run, remember?"

"So? Call him. Spill it all out over the phone."

My face must've showed my scepticism, because Safia got up in my face, fiercer than I'd seen her in a long time. "Do it. Life is short, Rama. We know this better than anyone. Who cares if it's over the phone? Tell him again when he gets back if you like. Tell him a thousand times. Just don't make him spend another second believing you don't love him."

The cynic in me thought she was being ridiculous, but that part of me was small, and shrinking by the day the longer I spent on this fucking mountain. In my heart, I knew she was right. Fen was out there somewhere after spending the night in my bed, inside *me*, and he had no clue how I felt about him.

That had to change.

Right now.

Ignoring Safia's giddy smile, I ducked past her and slipped out of the kitchen, dashing back across the yard to make the most of the signal hot spot in the cabin. She'd handle Charlie if he woke and feed him a better breakfast than the Nutella on toast I'd planned.

The log cabin smelled of us. Of man and sweat and sex. I loved it. I breathed it in while searching the rumpled bed for my phone, collecting a stray condom wrapper for my trouble and dumping it into the bin.

My phone was on the floor, half hidden by a sock that wasn't mine. It was blue with a white snowflake woven into it and I knew instantly that it was Fen's, though I had no memory of him taking it off. Last night had been a blur of wild energy and happiness, the details weren't important. All that mattered was letting him know how much it had meant to me.

How much *he* meant to me.

I folded the sock and placed it on the bedside table. Then I swiped at my phone and made the call.

It rang three times before I heard his voice, crackly and gruff, the sound of big machinery at work in the background.

I laughed. "Is this a bad time?"

"What?"

"A bad time," I repeated. "I can call back later."

Fen said something.

I missed it. "Huh?"

Silence. And then he laughed too, deep and rich. "I'm trying to tell you—"

He cut out again. For a moment, I thought he'd gone, then the line rattled to life again and his voice was louder.

Clearer.

"I don't know how much of that you caught, but I'm trying to tell you I love you."

"Fen—"

"No, don't say anything. I don't need you to. I just want you to know that whatever you decide to do, I support you. And Charlie. Hell, I'll drive to Manchester and back every day if that's what you need, just...damn, just don't walk away from—"

He cut out again, and this time, he didn't come back. I called a couple of times, but the line was dead. Wherever he was, the signal was worse than it was up here, and that was saying something.

Still, even losing contact with him did nothing to dull the shiny joy rising in my chest. *He loves me.* I'd already known it in some way or other, but to hear him say it did things to me I'd never experienced before. My eyes burned and my heart swelled, and maybe, just maybe, for the first time since Charlie had been born, the practicalities really didn't matter.

Not yet.

He loves me.

Jesus fuck, I loved him too.

And I'd failed in my mission to let him know, a realisation that had me reaching for my phone again.

A message waited for me. I'd missed it buzzing through while I'd been lost in a goddamn love bubble. Who the hell was I right now?

Exactly who you were always meant to be.

My mother didn't come to me very often, but in that moment, her voice was clear as the air at the top of Christmas Mountain.

I opened the message.

Fen: *sorry, this motorway might as well be the moon. i'll tell you it all again when i get home—tonight, maybe. or the morning if we run out of driving hrs xx*

God, I hoped it was tonight, but the morning wasn't a lifetime away either. Blowing out a breath, I tapped out a reply.

Rami: *Be safe. Got lots to tell you too. All of it good. Can't wait to see you xxx*

The message fired off, but didn't deliver for a while. I put the phone down and set about putting the room back together after our hot night in. The bed was a write-off. I stripped the sheets and put new ones on, then I shook out the rug and swept the fireplace. There wasn't much I could do about the new squeak in the bed without crawling beneath it with an allen key and some WD40, and life was too short for that.

I took the bedclothes to the house. It was raining again, heavy sheets of water that swept across the yard, soaking me to the skin the brief few seconds I was outside.

Safia laughed. "You'll have to toughen up if you're gonna live up here."

"I'm plenty tough, thanks, mate." I shook my hair out to prove it, flicking water in her face. It earned me another shove, harder this time, but I didn't care. She could shove me all day long. Fen loved me, I loved him, and everything was perfect.

I spent the rest of the day hiding from the rain. Christmas was a week away and I'd yet to buy a single present, but I distracted myself from that by eating every sausage roll Safia had made for the freezer and helping the kids replace the edible decorations they'd pinched from the tree.

Addie made shortbread spaceships. Mae made reindeers. Charlie crafted inedible lumps he'd licked a thousand times before they'd even baked, but that was life.

My life, and I loved it.

The afternoon came and went. And then the evening. Fen didn't text again, but the horrific weather had caused chaos on the motorways down south, so I gave up on expecting him back before dawn and went to bed kind of wishing I'd left the sex-rumpled sheets in place.

The earth shifted as I floated off to sleep. At least, I

thought it did, but I was tired enough to believe it was an imaginary goodnight from Fen and I smiled as I slipped into dreamland.

Like a kid waiting for Christmas, I was convinced the night would last forever, but morning came faster than I was prepared for.

I jumped awake, heart slamming against my ribcage, not knowing what had woken me.

Grumbling, I rubbed my face and flopped back, but my eyes seemed to be wired open, despite the fact that it was barely light outside, and I found myself *itching* to get out of bed. Goddamn, what had happened to me on this fucking mountain?

You fell in love.

You found a home.

Sweet, right? Man, if I hadn't felt so good about it, it would've been nauseating as hell.

Cynic.

Retired, as it went. It was hard to feel pessimistic about much right then.

I slid out of bed and dressed in the warm clothes I'd brought from Manchester. I'd need a flannel shirt or two if I was going to fit in around here, but as much as I loved Fen, I wasn't there yet. I was still accepting that butt-ugly boots were now my number one choice of footwear.

Out of habit, I reached for my phone and distractedly swiped at the screen while I stamped into said boots. I hadn't counted on hearing from Fen and my heart leapt at the message flashed across the screen.

Fen: *gave up in Birmingham and parked the rig. getting a taxi back to the depot and driving home to get some kip. see you at sunrise baby x*

Sunrise. I glanced at the window. The misty early morning was fast giving way to clear skies, the winter sun powering through the clouds yesterday's rain had left behind.

I crouched to tie my laces, then hurried outside, still zipping my coat against the bitter wind. I wasn't expecting to see anyone, save maybe Fen lounging against his Land Rover like a lumberjack god on a magazine cover.

Paddy's tall frame sprinting across the yard caught me off guard. "All right, mate. Where's the fire?"

He skidded to a stop, lurching around to face me. His face was ashen. Eyes wide. "Did you hear it? In the night?"

"Hear what?" The warmth in my heart cooled, drowned out by icy dread. "What's wrong?"

"Landslide. The road's gone, and..." He stopped and glanced back over his shoulder, panic searing his usually open gaze.

His distress hit me like a ton of bricks, and I closed the distance between us, grabbing his arm and digging my fingers into his flesh like torture devices. "What? *What?* Goddamn it, just tell me."

Paddy swallowed hard. "Rama, I can't see Fen's house."

16

Rami

The world stopped. My breath, my heart, my brain, as if everything I was and everything I wanted to be had never existed at all.

I stared at Paddy, terror squeezing my chest. "What do you mean you can't see his fucking house?"

"Exactly what I said," Paddy snapped. He wrenched free of my grasp and took off again, heading for the mountain path that led to the treehouse.

I stood frozen, caught between following him and charging back the way he'd come to see for myself what had sucked the blood from his face.

I need to see it.

Heart in my mouth, I ran to the gate and launched myself over it, landing like a cat in the soggy ground on the other side. Mud stuck to my boots like clay, sucking my feet into the quagmire, but nothing could hold me down. I pounded the earth, eating up the distance between my sister's home and the point on the mountain road where Fen's cosy house should've been visible.

It wasn't, but denial kept me moving. Paddy was taking the piss. It was a bad joke. The fucking worst. Or he was plain wrong. He had to be. Landslides happened on TV—in movies and on the news in places with better landscapes than this. They didn't happen on Christmas Mountain.

They *couldn't*.

The thought carried me to the bend in the road that looked out over the horizon. Then the road disappeared, crumbling down the side of the fell in a mass of brown and grey, broken trees piled high in a messy slag heap below... where Fen's house had once stood.

No. I stumbled, sinking to my knees in the claggy dirt. *It's okay. Maybe he didn't make it back yet. Maybe he got stuck in traffic on the way home and never made it up the mountain.* But even as the rationale screamed through my mind, my gaze fell on the twisted metal of an upturned car.

Fen's car.

He'd made it home.

But he hadn't made it out.

Another strangled sound escaped me. I fell forward, my hands joining my knees in the mud. *No.* This couldn't be fucking happening.

It *wasn't* fucking happening.

I scrambled to my feet and sprinted back the way I'd come, leaving the ruined, impassable road behind. Paddy was long gone, but I knew where he'd headed—to the disused path behind the tree house that led into the forest. The one he and Fen both had warned me to leave well alone. With the road blocked, it was the only way down the mountain that didn't require rock-climbing gear.

I'd never been much of a runner. Martial arts and sex had been my exercise of choice for most of my adult life. But I flew over the ground now, my feet barely touching the dirt beneath me, and I was on Paddy before I could reconcile with the hell I'd woken up to.

His expression hadn't changed. "There's no way down," he said. "The whole fell is totally fucked."

"Define fucked."

"We can't get down," he repeated, as if my face was telling him I didn't understand. Or that something deep inside me was refusing to try. "I've been calling Fen, but it's not connecting, not even to the landline. Safia was calling the main house when I ran out."

We dashed back up the mountain. Safia was on the doorstep, phone in hand, Lalla strapped in a sling on her chest. "Nothing's working." She flitted a wide-eyed stare to me. "You think it took out the mast?"

"Depends how far down it went," Paddy said. "Who else can we call?"

"No one if our phones aren't fucking working."

Paddy turned away from Safia's frustration and jogged back to the gate. He scanned the horizon, shoulders tense. "Rama, try your phone."

It was still in the cabin. I ran for it and called Fen as soon as I picked it up, ignoring Paddy who'd trailed me across the yard. For a long moment, nothing happened, then the line crackled to life and it rang.

Once.

And cut out.

"Mother*fucker.*" I twitched, ready to hurl the phone at the wall.

The thought of Fen trying to call back checked me.

Breathing hard, I called him again and again and again. Nothing happened, not even a flicker, and I returned to Paddy with a heavy heart. "It rang once, now it's dead."

"At least something's working, though," Paddy grunted. "Try the house."

"Which house? His?"

"Yeah. And the main house. One of the guys might pick up."

Wishful thinking. Apparently that one ring was all we had. Every other call failed to connect, and then my phone lost signal. On shaky legs, I charged back to the treehouse and climbed the stairs to connect to the satellite Internet, but calls to Fen's phone and any other numbers Paddy could think of still wouldn't connect.

Trepidation filled my heart as I logged into my laptop and searched a local news site. Images of the dislodged earth at the foot of the mountain filled the screen, but the reports held no information of the fate of anyone above, only that any search and rescue operations were being hampered by inclement weather.

I glowered out of the window. The sky as far as I could see was crystal clear. "What inclement weather?" I growled. "It's a fucking spring day out there."

"It's cold," Paddy said. "The wet ground is going to be ice soon enough. Even if the road was useable, they'd need specialist vehicles to make it to Fen's place."

"To *Fen*, you mean. Who gives a fuck about his house?"

"You don't know he was inside."

"His car was there. Where else would he be?" I was

verging on hysterical, and in the short time it had taken to waking up on cloud nine to landing in this nightmare, I hadn't given Charlie a second thought. "Fuck. I need to get Charlie."

"Easy." Paddy gripped my elbow with his giant hand. "Saf's got the kids. It's what we do now, remember? We're in this together."

Together. The word felt hollow. I'd sold myself a dream on this goddamn mountain with Fen by my side. Imagining this life without him *hurt*.

So fucking much.

I stumbled to the futon we'd got down and dirty on a few days after I'd taken his father's office as my own. It didn't feel real—none of it did. The good, the bad, and downright fucking awful. *Am I still asleep? Have I been dreaming this whole fucking time and I'm going to wake up miserable and alone in Manchester without him still?*

The thought made my stomach churn, and for a painful second I thought I'd puke. Then something shut off inside me. A kill switch I couldn't control. Numbness descended, dark and consuming. I stood and drifted to the window again, but instead of Mother Nature's carnage kicked out before me, I saw nothing.

Felt nothing.

Said nothing.

Paddy was silent too. He joined me at the window for a while, then he gripped my elbow again. "Come on. Let's go back to the house and try the phones again."

"I should stay here in case the Internet picks something up."

"Fine. I'll get the kids then."

He backed off and disappeared. I listened to his footsteps

on the stairs fade out, but didn't break my stare off with the clear blue sky.

It seemed like no time at all had passed when he came back, a sleepy Charlie in his arms, the other kids clinging to his legs.

Safia was behind him, holding Lalla. She read the room and retreated to the futon. Paddy backed up to the corner and sat on the floor with Charlie in his lap, using every phone we had to place calls that went nowhere.

The kids stayed with me.

Mae tugged my sleeve. "Uncle Rama?"

"Yeah?"

"Are we stuck here because the mountain fell over?"

It was the most innocent question this sharp-edged kid had ever asked. I bent to her level. Opened my mouth, but nothing came out.

I shook my head. "I, uh, I don't know, bug."

"We should stay up here then. I like it in here. It smells like you and biscuits."

She didn't ask me about Fen. Neither did Addie, despite the fact they'd witnessed nothing but panic since they'd woken up. Mae's little hand was warm in mine and I clung to it as I sat on the floor opposite Paddy.

We didn't look at each other. He ran out of phone calls to make and a tense, pensive silence settled over us for the next few hours.

Hours that felt like days.

I leaned against the wall, eyes half-closed, brain whirring with an inefficient mechanism that served no purpose at all. It was white noise. Dull static. It was a black fucking hole, and I sank so far into it I barely noticed Addie scrambling to his feet at some point where the sun had long since passed its highest point. It didn't register, even when he shouted and pressed his face against the glass.

Not until he banged it with his miniature fists and yelled my name. "Rama! Uncle Rama. Look! It's Fen. He's falling *up* the mountain."

17

Fen

Man, I considered myself as hardy as my hardiest tree, but after an entire day up to my knees in freezing, wet mud, I was cold to the bone. I couldn't feel my feet, my hands, or my brain. The only part of me that was truly working was my anxious heart.

Get to Rami. Get to Safia and the kids. Make sure they're okay.

At first, I'd taken comfort in the single ring my cracked and smashed phone had registered from Rami. Then, as the day had gone on and no further sign of life had come down from the mountain, I'd started to panic. What if he'd been calling for help?

Worse, what if he'd been hurt and someone else had been calling to tell me?

Don't catastrophise. You already know the landslip started further down.

Yeah, but—

Stop.

And I had to. My thoughts were too jumbled to make any sense. All I could do was put one foot in front of the other until the precarious path I'd staggered upside Christmas Mountain evened out into something that didn't try to kill me every other step.

Rami. Get to Rami.

My foot caught on a rock. I pitched forward, hands hitting the deck for the umpteenth time. My palms were bloody and raw, at least, they looked it. Cold, remember? I couldn't feel a thing.

Dazed, I came upright and kept moving, still waiting for the mountain to be kind to me. I tripped again and sighed as I went down like a sack of spuds. The fear that had carried me this far was muted, and I waited for the sharp impact of the ground. Pain was pain. It meant you were alive, right? And as long as I was alive, I had Rami.

I *loved* Rami. I'd tumble down this mountain a thousand times if I reached him on my next attempt.

But I didn't fall. The bruising impact I'd resigned myself to never came and instead of a face full of dirt, I found myself spinning and spinning and spinning until I opened my eyes to a gruff curse, and the sweetest brown gaze I'd ever seen.

"Jesus fuck, you look like you've been in a landslide."

In my hazy brain, it was hard to discern a couple of things. One: if Rami was genuinely annoyed. Two: if he was even real. A lazy chuckle fell out of me, distant and low. "I think I woke up in a landslide."

"Are you awake now?"

"You tell me."

Rami said something I didn't catch, then my weight shifted and my feet didn't feel like bricks anymore.

I couldn't tell you what happened next. Just that the

mountain disappeared. The cold ground gave way to rustic wooden floorboards, the frigid air to a roaring fireplace, and my hands regained sensation around a mug of something that smelt of chocolate and whisky.

Rami's face solidified too. What I'd mistaken for anger was something else—something I recognised as the emotion that had carried me up the fell: fear. The real stuff, the kind that gripped your soul until something wonderful made it go away.

I put the mug down and reached for Rami, aiming for his face, but my cold-addled hands landed on his shoulders instead.

He caught them, squeezing them tight, and leaned close enough that I could smell him, that cinnamon and mystery scent that wasn't so mysterious anymore. He smelt different now; dry humour, earnest compassion, and love. I'd told him I loved him, right? In between being stuck on a lorry for nineteen hours and waking up to forest dystopia, I was doubting everything.

"Fen."

I blinked.

Rami said my name again and released my hands to cup my face in his warm palms. "Never mind. You can tell me later. But can *I* tell *you* something before you fall asleep on me?"

"I'm not asleep."

"Whatever. I love you, and I need you to know that."

My head jerked up from where it had been fast descending to my chest hard enough to give me whiplash. "What?"

Rami laughed. "I said, I fucking *love* you. And I'm sorry you didn't know it until now."

A beat of silence settled between us. My brain jolted to life, my heart too, but the rest of me wouldn't comply. My eyes were so heavy it felt like they were melting into my face and I couldn't quite believe that those sweet, sweet words were meant for me.

"Lie down," Rami whispered.

"What?"

"Down," he repeated with a hint of authority that would've heated my blood in circumstances that weren't so bemusing. "You're exhausted. We can talk later. Just know that I love you, Fen. Nothing else matters right now."

▲

I came to on the couch in Paddy and Safia's cosy living room, curled up between Rami's long legs, my head on his chest. His gentle fingers were tangled in my hair, and Charlie was using my thigh as a bench while he watched cartoons and ate a jam tart.

A deep rumble sounded from my belly. I laughed and Rami snapped his gaze to me. "You're awake."

"I am." I secured Charlie and sat up, sliding him into my lap. "What time is it?"

"Somewhere around half past what in the ever loving *fuck* happened to you?"

"Oh."

"Yeah. Oh. Want to tell me how you came to be deliriously wandering Christmas Mountain with blood dripping down your face?"

"Huh?"

Rami took my hand and raised it to my cheekbone. A sharp sting met my touch. I hissed. "I forgot about that."

"And your hands too?"

I glanced at my hands. They were grubby and covered in cuts. "I fell...I think. Up the mountain."

"I know that much," Rami said. "We saw you. Well, Addie did. I thought you were dead, so..."

"You'd given up on me?"

"Never. It was more I couldn't see how you could've possibly made it out of your house."

"My house?"

"Yup. It's completely buried."

I nodded. "It is."

"Were you in it at the time?"

"You sure you want to know?"

Rami grimaced. "Seeing as you're alive and well, I think I can probably cope, but I'm not going to like it."

"Why not?"

"Because I fucking love you, that's why."

So it hadn't been a dream. He loved me. Even if he hadn't uttered the words, I could see it in his shiny gaze and earnest smile. *He loves me.* Damn. Maybe that was why it hadn't sunk in that I'd probably lost my house. *I'm homeless, but he loves me.* It was a fair trade, in my eyes. Everything else could be replaced.

"You're grinning hard enough to give yourself a stroke." Rami nudged me. "I meant what I said earlier, though."

"Which part?"

"The part about being sorry that I didn't get to tell you before the signal cut out yesterday. It's why I called in the first place."

"You called to tell me you love me?"

"And that I'm not leaving. I'd have meant that too if I'd managed to say it."

"Not leaving," Charlie echoed, sleepy eyes still fixed on the TV.

I ruffled his hair, noting that I was somehow dressed in Paddy's clothes as I processed the influx of my wildest dreams coming true. A slow smile grew on my face, but it was cautious. Disbelieving, almost. The last twenty-four hours had been carnage. Was I lucky enough to wake up from that to this? "Say all that again," I said gruffly.

Rami sat up. He shifted Charlie from my lap and whispered in his ear.

Charley giggled and wandered off, calling Paddy's name. Rami watched him go until he was happy with wherever he'd ended up, then he turned back to me with an expression so open I fell into it and drowned. "We're staying, Fen. I gave my notice at the probation service and I'm going to set up a remote counselling service for young offenders when I'm done with my last cases. It's what's best for Charlie, and best for me, even without the fact that I think I'm falling head over heels in love with you."

"You *think*?"

Rami chuckled. "I *know*. I was trying to be cool."

"What the hell for?"

"So I didn't scare you back to sleep. I missed you while you were gone."

There was humour in his words, but a deeper emotion too. He was speaking the truth. He loved me.

And I loved him.

I exhaled a quiet breath. "I've wanted this all along. I know it's fast and sudden and probably a little crazy, but I think I knew how I felt about you the moment you got out of that car. Like it was fate, you know? That everything that had happened to both of us had brought us to that point for a reason—for *this* reason."

"I've never believed in stuff like that." Rami traced a random pattern on the back of my hand. "But I do now. And I don't care that it's fast. I'm tired of waiting for life to happen to me and dealing with other people's bullshit instead. I want this. I want *you*, and me, and Charlie together for as long as it works, and you never fucking know. It could be forever."

I liked the sound of that. I pulled Rami close and kissed his temple, revelling in the sensation of his lean, unyielding body against my bulk. I was bigger than him, stronger perhaps, but only in the physical sense. He was my hero, and I couldn't wait to spend forever with him.

Rami let me hold him for a while, but it wasn't long before he pushed back and returned us to the subject of the muddy apocalypse that had nearly stolen this moment from us. "What the *fuck* happened? We woke up to find your house buried, your car sticking arse end out of the mud, and no path down the fell to get to you. I never gave up on you, not for a second, but *jesus*, I was scared." He shuddered. "So fucking scared."

"I was too, especially when I saw the state of my bedroom. I'd nearly asked you to bring Charlie down and wait for me there. If you had, well..." I shook my head. "Let's just say I'm glad I dozed off on the couch and leave it at that."

Rami arched a brow. "Don't be vague with me. I have an overactive imagination, so I'd prefer the truth."

"Me too." Safia entered the room and perched on the arm of the couch. "And I already spoke to Daryl at the main house, so don't even think of giving us the diet version."

I sighed. "Really?"

"Really," she snapped. "You were family long before you

were boinking my brother, and we were terrified we'd lost you."

Rami pursed his lips, half cringing, half hiding a grin.

I didn't know what to say.

To any of it.

So I went with the truth. "I didn't hear it coming. I woke up to find half my house buried and I couldn't get out. My phone was smashed up and not working and I couldn't reach the landline. My lads from the farm came looking for me and dug me out. As soon as I knew they were okay too, I made a run for it to get to you guys, but the paths were all ruined. I think it took me longer to get up here than it did to get out of my house."

"It took you six hours," Paddy said, joining us with every child hanging off him. There was felt-tip scribble on his forehead. I wondered if Rami had told Charlie to put it there. "They thought you'd lost the plot, but Safia told them you'd be right as rain after a hot dinner and nap."

"She was right, about the nap part, at least. I feel fine." Better than fine. I was on top of the world in every sense. At some point, I'd have to face some difficult realities about the state of my house, and the fact that half of next year's timber had likely been destroyed, but that could wait. All of it could. As long as my guys still had jobs, here and now—that was what mattered.

Safia came closer and gave me a hug. She was built like Rami—compact, but deceptively strong. She squeezed the life out of me, stealing my breath, then fixed me with another stern gaze. "I don't know what your intentions are with my sweet brother—"

Rami snorted.

Safia thumped him and continued, "—but whatever they

are, there's no way you can live in that house for the foreseeable future so you're moving in with us, no arguments."

I opened my mouth.

Paddy cut me off. "No arguments, dude. Right, kids?"

Addie nodded.

Mae gave me a bored stare. "I don't want to argue with you because I already did stuff today so you should just live here forever."

Rami's snort gave way to full-on laughter, and it coincided with the timed lights on the Christmas tree flickering to life, casting the room in a warm glow that felt like a hug from all of them.

Living here, with Safia and Paddy. Their kids. Charlie. With *Rami*. Wow. The carnage. The joy.

The love.

Had Christmas come early?

I guessed I was about to find out.

I nodded, my hand reaching for Rami of its own accord as Charlie left Paddy and toddled to the couch to plonk himself in a position that left him draped over Rami and me both.

It seemed kind of fitting.

I had no words but three, and they were all for Rami. "I love you."

18

Rami

Christmas Eve

It was my last ever call as a probation officer. My notice was scheduled to run for another month, but my boss had put me on gardening leave, gifting me precious time to get my shit together on full pay.

Right now, I didn't have much to complain about, and it apparently showed on my face.

The Zoom call connected. The last offender in my care took one look at me and rolled his eyes.

He didn't say anything, but this offender rarely did. He listened more than he spoke, saw more than most people realised, and I was going to miss his penetrating scowl.

I ran through the information he needed to navigate the end of his probation, then I kicked back in my chair, signalling to him that the formalities were over.

His expression didn't change, but I was used to that. He

gave me little, but it was still a thousand times more than he gave anyone else.

He humoured my small talk and I knew I should let him go, but something drove me to keep him on the line. *Perhaps you're not as ready as you thought to leave this job behind.*

No. That wasn't it. I'd ruminated it to death and I was done. Charlie was my priority. Fen. My family. I loved my work, but that was all it was. Work. It didn't warm my bed at night, or torment me at rowdy family dinners. It was over. I was done.

I opened my mouth to say so, but activity behind me caught my attention. Footsteps on the stairs, the door opening.

Fuck. I sat up, ready to kill the screen, but my agitation died as Fen stepped into the office. Still, I held up a hand to warn him off. Dante Pope had left prison expecting never to see Fen Hawthorne again. I had to honour that, or at least give him the choice.

Fen frowned, keeping his gaze away from my laptop screen. "Shit. Sorry. I thought you'd be done."

I should've been. He'd done exactly as I'd asked and left me in peace until six o'clock, and now here we were, stuck in an awkward-as-fuck situation that I could only fix by hanging up on Dante or kicking Fen out.

Or...

No. I couldn't do that. Last day or not, it was inappropriate as hell. And serious TMI for an offender who likely gave zero fucks about my private life.

"Hey Fen."

I snapped my gaze back to my laptop. Dante was still sitting on the same stone steps he had been when he'd taken my call. The same Christmas roses and camellias were behind him—I knew what the blooms were called because he'd told me about them in enough detail to make me grin like a Cheshire cat. His smirk was different, though. Warmer and more open than I'd ever seen him be with anyone but his boyfriend.

"I recognised his voice," he said to my obvious confusion. "It's nice that you're together now."

"Um—"

"Hey Pope." Fen joined me at the screen. He raised a hand in a half wave and gave Dante an intense once-over and whatever he saw seemed to be enough. He nodded. Dante nodded back, and that was it.

Dante's smirk widened enough to be a genuine smile, and then he was gone.

The blank screen he left behind shocked me. I sat back in my seat again, blowing out a breath.

Fen rubbed my shoulders. "Going to miss him?"

"No. Maybe. I don't know. Sorry about that. I ran over."

Fen snorted. "I figured. It was nice to see him, though. You never forget some of them, do you?"

"Nope. Did it sound weird to you when he said it was nice that we were together? Why would he assume that just because you were in my office? I never told him I was working from home."

"Um..." Fen darted a shifty gaze around the room, then gave me a sheepish smile. "He clocked my crush on you about a million years ago. He thought we were already together, actually, and it kind of gave me the push to ask you out that time."

"I'd have said yes, you know that, right? If I'd made it back to the prison before you got hurt? Maybe if I had—"

Fen cut me off with a soft kiss, his cobalt-blue eyes

swimming with warmth and love. "It doesn't matter. None of it does. We're here now."

I couldn't argue with that. I shut down my laptop for the rest of the year and let Fen lead me out of the treehouse and up the mountain. The ground was icy and cold, the dampness from the torrential rain long gone. I still looked at the forest floor with suspicion, though. Fen seemed to have moved past the fact that he'd lost another of his nine lives, but I remained half-convinced that Durdle Fell wasn't done with us yet.

Cynic. Maybe. But I was getting better at that, and with Fen by my side, I was a stronger man than I'd ever been.

We reached the house and slipped inside. Charlie had just got out of the bath. Fen took him to the Christmas tree and told him a fable about the forest creatures that had roamed the land before us.

I was spellbound.

Charlie fell asleep.

Fen shook his head. "At least I'm soothing, eh?"

"You're more than that."

The room filled up before I could elaborate, but it didn't matter. Fen knew how I felt. I'd told him more than once since we'd found him stumbling up the fell, covered in mud and blood, and I'd tell him again before the night was over.

Mince pies, too much spiced wine, and terrible comedy took up the rest of the evening. We hung the stockings and chased the older kids to bed, then left Paddy and Safia to keep them there, retreating to the log cabin that was to be our home while Fen's house was being repaired.

I'm living with a bloke I'm not related to.

It was a reality I'd never imagined when I'd thrown myself into my piece-of-shit car and hurled Charlie and me up Christmas Mountain, but sometimes real life was better than dreams.

I squeezed Fen's hand as we stepped inside the cabin. "Did you rescue the photographs?"

Fen gave me a broad grin. "Yup. Every single one. I'm beginning to think I'm blessed by the mountain gods. I only lost material things I don't care about. That has to mean something."

I knew what it meant—it meant that Mother Nature knew as well as I did that Fen had suffered enough. That he was a good, kind man who deserved the fucking world. But I kept that to myself. Fen wasn't a man who could be told what he was worth and believe it. And he didn't need to be. He just needed to know he was loved, and by now I was hoping he did.

It was late. Though we hadn't been sharing a room for long, we moved around each other in perfect synch as we got ready for bed. Fen liked the window cracked open—northern weirdo—and I didn't care. And I liked the smile on his face when I remembered to open it before we slid into bed. Loved it, actually. Perhaps it was the festive excitement lacing the air, but there wasn't much I didn't like right now. Everything seemed brighter, even the sun, and I was beginning to worry I'd pull a muscle in my face from smiling so much.

Grinch.

"You've got your thinking face on." Fen tapped my temple. "It's cute."

I rolled over in the bed. Fen was bare-chested and glorious. He was my ultimate fantasy in every which way possible, but this was probably my favourite. "You think I'm cute."

"Always have."

"Was it the clothes? Because I hate to break it to you, but I'm burning my business casual threads and investing in flannel."

"You don't think I have enough for the both of us?"

"I don't know the depths of your obsession. Is it something I should be worried about?"

Fen laughed, like we both had so many times over the past few days, free and happy. "I guess you'll find out when I rescue my clothes from the house."

I guessed I would. We had a lot to learn about each other, but I was ready for the journey.

Fen leaned in and kissed me, sweet and gentle, but I was fast learning that there wasn't much sweet about him when it came to sex. Falling so hard for each other had apparently activated beast mode, and I wasn't complaining. I loved the feel of his bulk pressing me down, his big, work-hardened hands roaming my skin. I didn't need Fen to feel safe—it wasn't about that—but there was something so fucking soothing about the rough way he handled me.

He pushed me onto my back, making a cradle for himself between my legs. I fought the temptation to wrap them around him. *Not yet.* The last few days had been so hectic, I wanted to make the most of this quiet—for now—time with him. I wanted to sink into every kiss, every scratch of his unshaven jaw along mine, and every harsh snatch of breath he gasped in between.

We'd fallen into the habit of sleeping naked, and without the time it took to undress, Fen was inside me before long. He stretched me open with his cock, easing in with a gentleness that belied what would come next.

Heat sizzled in my blood, eclipsing the initial discomfort

of his big dick. I threw back my head and moaned, arching my back to take him deeper.

Fen chuckled. "Easy. We've got all night."

With any luck, we had far longer than that. But calming myself down while he was fucking me? Yeah. Wasn't happening, and not for the first time since half the mountain had fallen on top of his house, I was grateful to my sister for putting me up in a cabin away from the main house. At some point I'd have to learn to do this quietly, but I wasn't there yet.

I was light years away.

A thousand Christmasses.

Fen buried himself to the hilt and covered me with his body, pinning me to the bed. He drew his hips back, then snapped them forward, a sharp shot of pleasure that sent my eyes rolling in my skull. He was good at that—so fucking good.

He fucked me slowly, but with a brutal edge that took me apart so fast I wasn't prepared for the climax that snuck up on me.

I resisted it, just, digging my fingers into Fen's shoulders.

He laughed, breathless, and fucked me harder, and for long minutes, he had the upper hand. Fen had learned how to take me to the edge over and over without seeming to lose his composure.

But I knew better. I'd studied him as much as he'd studied me, and I recognised the signs that his control was slipping— his hooded gaze, his bottom lip caught in his teeth. The darkening flush on his chest. I watched his jaw unhinge and made my move, wrapping my legs around his waist, hooking him closer. I shoved my hand into his hair and yanked him down, taking his mouth in a bruising kiss as I thrust my hips up to meet his.

We collided. Raw desire sluiced through me and what had begun as a slow endeavour became frenetic enough to bang the bed against the wall.

Fen's arms began to shake, his thick biceps trembling as he fought to hold himself up. I went in for the kill, tightening my body around him, but I took the bullet first.

Release screamed through me, lighting a new fire in my already scorched veins. I came without touching my dick, and it was another out-of-body experience. Only watching Fen fall off the same cliff kept me tethered to the world.

His movements slowed, but didn't stop, as if something primal inside him was unwilling to let go yet.

I understood.

I felt the same.

But we had to stop. It was late and we'd both had long days, me in my office in the sky saying goodbye to the job that had been my life for a decade, him digging his worldly possessions out of his buried house. And it was Christmas Eve, a day that had never excited me before, but I was buzzing with anticipation now, and not just for the food.

And not for the presents. No one had got round to buying any, so it was going to be a day built from love and I couldn't fucking wait.

Fen cleaned us both up, then came back to the bed with the kind of smile that made me wonder how I'd got so lucky.

He lay on his side, facing me. I reached out and pushed his sweat-damp hair back. He hadn't had it cut since I'd turned his life upside down, and I liked the shaggy mess his ash-brown locks had become. I liked his scruffy jaw, his broad shoulders, and his enchanting eyes.

Most of all, I loved his overgrown heart.

"It's midnight," he whispered. "Merry Christmas."

I smiled. Again. An addiction I couldn't quit. "Merry Christmas."

🎄

Fen

One year later...*Christmas Day*

It was official: I was the worst cook in the family. But in my defence, the rest of them were so good I never stood a chance.

So I left them to it and played to my strengths—hauling wood, building fires, and making a mess with the kids in as many different ways as possible. We'd decorated the trees weeks ago. That's right—trees, plural. What was the point of having a Christmas tree farm if I couldn't fill my house and everyone else's with as many Nordic firs as would fit?

None. The fact that it gave my pint-sized partners in crime and myself an on-tap supply of gingerbread was an added bonus.

"All gone," Charlie sing-songed as I crammed the last one into my mouth.

"Yup." I swallowed it down and ruffled his hair. It had grown lighter in the past year, picking up natural highlights from the sun. He still had the Stone dark gaze, though, and he was as capable of hypnotising me as his uncle. "You still going to eat your dinner? I think Safia might kill me if you don't."

"I'll eat it, but no sprouts. Stinky."

Valid. With the trees razed of all things edible, we went back to playing the game we'd built during the Friday afternoon slot Rami and I took over Safia's home school. The huge wooden board was as chaotic and colourful as the disordered shambles we created every week, and engrossed us so much I didn't hear footsteps behind me.

Lean arms snaked around my waist, soft lips brushing my neck, and then the subtle, gentle scrape of teeth that made my knees weak. "Who's winning?"

"No idea. I can't remember the rules."

Rami chuckled. "I told you to write them down."

"Where's the fun in that?"

His answer was more laughter, and it was a sound that would never get old. We split our time between the homestead at the top of the mountain and the house we'd rebuilt half way down, but it didn't matter where we were, two things remained constant: laughter and love.

Sometimes, it was hard to believe my life was real.

Christmas Day passed like the last—so fast I mourned it when it was over. The only thing I didn't miss was Safia's obsession with surrogacy.

"You can tell her to stop," Rami said when we were naked in our log cabin bed, a place I'd come to see as my home as much as anywhere else on Christmas Mountain. "I'm not saying she would, but at least she'd know it's making you uncomfortable."

I snapped my gaze up from where I'd been exploring his chest with my tongue. "Uncomfortable? Say what?"

Rami let his molten eyes bore into me. "You cringe every time she mentions it. I figured it was freaking you out."

"It is, but not like that."

Rami arched a brow. He was good at making people talk —he had to be, in his line of work running a remote counselling programme from his office in the sky—and he didn't even have to try with me. One look and everything came pouring out.

I shifted up the bed to lie next to him. "I don't hate the idea. I'm cringing because I don't want her banging on about it to make you think it's something we have to do. Something I need to be happy. Because it's not."

"You want to have more kids?"

"It's not as tangible as that. I just—I don't know. I wouldn't think twice if you wanted it too, that's what I'm saying."

Rami frowned, but it wasn't a bad frown. It was speculative. Curious. And I knew that the future held the kind of conversations he was so good at. The serious ones that scared other people, but never, ever him.

Christ, I love him.

We stopped talking. Kissed, touched, and fucked. Sometimes we lost whole nights to each other like this, but after a full-on festive day, that wasn't happening tonight. I moved inside Rami, my palm wrapped around his cock, until he groaned and spilled in my hand. Then I came so hard I swore louder than Rami, before we fell asleep as wrapped up in each other as we'd been when we woke that morning.

Dawn came fast. I opened my eyes to a crisp Boxing Day morning, clear skies, frost on the ground, sparkly icicles hanging from the trees.

There was also a sticky, chubby hand pawing my face. *Charlie.* Little menace had developed a habit of letting himself out of the main house in the morning and trotting over to the cabin. Paddy had installed every device he could think of to contain him, but somehow Charlie Houdini still made his escape and woke me. Yeah, that's right. Just me. I was the soft touch, apparently, and I was okay with that.

More than okay. I scooped him up and slid out of the bed

so we wouldn't wake Rami, grateful I'd prepared for this moment and yanked some underwear on before we'd passed out. I sat Charlie on the window ledge and pressed my finger to my lips. "Shh."

I dressed and stepped into my boots, then I hustled him out of the cabin to his favourite place on the mountain—the rope swing my dad had built me when I wasn't much older than him. The landslide had uprooted the tree it had hung from and deposited it on the roof of my house. A couple of weeks later, I'd brought it up here for the next generation of Christmas Mountain to enjoy.

Charlie was still little enough that he had to ride it on my lap and we swung back and forth for untold time until I sensed Rami's presence in the frosty forest glade.

I let Charlie down. He ran towards Rami but got distracted on the way, collecting the pine cones we used for eco-friendly kindling.

Rami rolled his eyes and hugged me instead. "I think he loves you more."

"Doubtful. You're his hero."

"Only because I have the final say in how much chocolate he gets to eat."

I slid my gaze sideways, as if I didn't let all the kids eat whatever they wanted whenever they wanted it.

Rami punched my arm.

Cute.

"So..." He glanced at Charlie, then focused on me. "I wanted to ask you something."

"Oh yeah? Are you gonna propose? Because I'm not wearing a suit to the wedding. My days of posh shoes and ironing shirts are over."

"I'd totally propose just to make you dress up like a penguin, but...no. That's not it."

I knew it wouldn't be. Neither one of us had any interest in marriage. It worked for other people, but we didn't need it. We had each other.

"It's related, though," Rami said. "Kind of."

"Okay. Now I'm intrigued."

"It's about Charlie. Now I've officially adopted him, I was wondering how you felt about having parental responsibility for him. You know, in case anything ever happened to me."

Nope. Not thinking about that. I skipped ahead to the next part. "What about Safia and Paddy?"

Rami shook his head. "I want you. And so does Charlie. He asks me all the time if you're his dad too, and I'm sick of telling him no when I don't mean it."

My heart had been thrumming with new life since I'd trudged out of my house to find him stranded on my driveway, but there was something else about the way it surged as his words sank in. "You want me to be his parent...legally?"

"I do." Rami fixed me with a steady stare. "For loads of reasons that you already know, but also because I want all the kids we have to be the same."

"You want to have more kids with me?"

"Yes, dammit. Are you going to repeat everything I say as if you don't have a fucking clue where this is coming from?"

Was I? Christ, I had no idea. All I knew for certain was that my wildest dreams were slowly coming true, one by one, piece by piece.

Christmas by Christmas.

"Are you crying? Rami stepped impossibly closer and rubbed his thumbs beneath my eyes.

I swatted him away. "Maybe. Don't make fun of me."

"I would never."

"Liar."

"Yeah, but only about that."

And God, didn't I know it? Rami was the most beautifully brutally honest soul I'd ever met.

He was the love of my life, and as I swept him off his feet so entirely Charlie screamed with laughter, Christmas Mountain felt more like home than it ever had.

▲

FURTHER READING: If you are interested in Dante Pope, his story is told in SALVATION, the third book of the Darkest Skies series. You'll also get to see Rami and Fen at work.

If you enjoyed this Christmas novel, you may like my others, HOMETOWN CHRISTMAS and ANGELS IN THE CITY.

▲

WANT MORE RAMI AND FEN? Yeah, me too, so I wrote a bonus scene you can collect when you sign up for my NEWSLETTER. If you already subscribe, this little beauty will hit your inbox on release day.

▲

All my bonus scenes are extended on my Patreon account which you can subscribe to HERE.

ABOUT THE AUTHOR

Right now, Instagram is the best way to keep up with Garrett. Click on the icon below to follow, or search @garrett_leigh

Bonus Material available for all books on Garrett's Patreon account. Includes short stories from Misfits, Slide, Strays, What Remains, Dream, and much more. Sign up here: https://www.patreon.com/garrettleigh

Facebook Fan Group, Garrett's Den... https://www.facebook.com/groups/garre...

Garrett is also an award winning cover artist, taking the silver medal at the Benjamin Franklin Book Awards in 2016. She designs for various publishing houses and independent authors at https://www.blackjazzdesign.com

Connect with Garrett
www.garrettleigh.com

ALSO BY GARRETT LEIGH

Info for all my books can be found on my website: http://www.garrettleigh.com

www.ingramcontent.com/pod-product-compliance
Lightning Source LLC
Chambersburg PA
CBHW020755190726
48285CB00006B/2047